Second Chances

GINNY WILLIAMS

HARVEST HOUSE PUBLISHERS
Eugene, Oregon 97402

SECOND CHANCES

Copyright © 1994 by Ginny Williams
Published by Harvest House Publishers
Eugene, Oregon 97402

Library of Congress Cataloging-in-Publication Data

Williams, Ginny, 1957–
    Second chances / Ginny Williams.
      p. cm. — (Class of 2000 ; bk. 1)
    Summary: When her father decides to remarry, fifteen-
year-old Kelly wonders why God has brought such turmoil into her
life, but then a beautiful black horse and a special friend bring her
new perspectives on those she loves.
    ISBN 1-56507-148-4
    [1. Remarriage—Fiction. 2. Horses—Fiction. 3. Christian
life—Fiction.] I. Title. II. Series: Williams, Ginny, 1957– Class
of 2000 ; bk. 1.
PZ7.W65919Se 1994   93-39061
[Fic]—dc20   CIP
                                       AC

Printed in the United States of America.

94 95 96 97 98 99 00 — 10 9 8 7 6 5 4 3 2 1

For my wonderful husband, Louis
Friends in Love Forever...

About the Author

Ginny Williams grew up loving and working with horses. When she got older, she added a love for teenagers to the top of her list. She admits she goes through withdrawal when she doesn't have kids around her, not that that has happened much in her fifteen years of youth ministry.

Ginny lives on a large farm outside of Richmond, Virginia, with her husband, Louis, two Labrador retrievers, a large flock of Canada geese, and a herd of deer. When she's not writing or speaking to youth groups, she can be found using her degree in recreation. She loves to travel and play. She bikes, plays tennis, windsurfs, rides horses (of course!), plays softball—she'll do anything that's fun! She's planning a bike trip across the country, and she's waiting for her chance to skydive and bungee jump.

O N E

Reaching over to shut the alarm clock off, Kelly waited breathlessly to see if anyone else would stir in response to the jangling noise. Hearing only silence, she let her breath out slowly and laid back in bed, enjoying the stillness of the morning. Spring had come early to the little town of Kingsport, North Carolina, that year. Even in this first week of March, the air was warm with the promise of Kelly's favorite season. She did not usually rise this early so she lay still, enjoying the music of the birds and the shafts of sunlight that were just beginning to peek through the arms of the tall oak stationed outside her second-story bedroom.

The sound of a truck backfiring as it wound its way on an early morning delivery route brought her thoughts sharply into focus. Today was the day— the day she had been dreading for months, the day she had hoped would never arrive. Her father was marrying that woman! Kelly had been sure that her father would come to his senses before he destroyed her life. Yet, Saturday, March 5, had arrived and on this day, at one o'clock, Peggy Landers would join

Scott Marshall as his wife. Kelly still couldn't believe her father was doing this to her.

Slowly she pulled herself out of bed, the beauty of the morning now ruined. Reaching into her closet she grabbed a pair of jeans that had seen better days and slid her slender body into them. They were followed quickly by her favorite red sweatshirt and a pair of beat-up tennis shoes. Slipping quietly into the bathroom, she dashed water into her face and ran a brush through her coppery curls. She looked more closely at her reflection in the mirror to see if it indicated devastation, but staring back were the same wide blue eyes, the same generous mouth, and the same pert nose sprinkled with freckles. Kelly made a face, marveling that anything could still be the same when her whole fifteen-year-old life was changing!

Quietly Kelly closed the heavy, oak front door as she moved from the house into the sunlight. Her father and her younger sister, Emily, were still sound asleep. If her timing was right, she would be back in plenty of time for breakfast. Pulling her bike from the garage, Kelly headed for the one place where she was sure she belonged—Porter's Riding Stables.

She had dragged herself out of bed so early this morning because she knew she would need the time at the barn to make it through the day. When her mother had died from cancer four years ago, Kelly had been comforted by the listening ears of her favorite horses. On the hardest days she would sit in the deep straw of their stalls and take comfort from their company while they ate. She needed her horses this morning.

Chewing on the thick piece of homemade bread she had grabbed as she passed through the kitchen, Kelly pedaled rapidly down the almost-deserted streets. Any other time she would have enjoyed the empty, early-morning fairways. She was dimly aware that the trees were sporting more of their soft, green spring wardrobe and that the ground underneath them was crowded with the red-breasted robins who had returned from their winter homes. Spring had always been a fascinating time of year to Kelly, but on this day she was dwelling only on the disaster about to happen.

The four years since her mother died had been hard ones, but Kelly, Emily, and her father had been okay. Struggling to make sense out of life without her mom, they had pulled together and developed a rare closeness. Even though Emily was four years younger, she and Kelly understood each other's sadness and loss and shared many of the same things. And Kelly considered her father her best friend. She always told him everything. If she felt life was unfair to have taken her mother at such an early age, she was also grateful for a father like hers. She had his coppery curly hair and his wide blue eyes, and she was proud that people knew she was Scott Marshall's daughter as soon as they saw her.

The road narrowed as she approached the drive to the stables. The oak trees seemed to form a protective canopy, as if they knew she was troubled. The thick covering broke the rays of sun into diamonds dancing along the pavement. The lush green pasture behind the sturdy rail fence was empty. All of the horses were in their stalls, enjoying their morning grain.

She had actually liked Peggy Landers at first, she remembered as she turned her bike down the barn drive. Widowed for three years herself and with no children to tie her down, Peggy had moved to Kingsport just a year ago to start a new life. She had gone to work in Scott Marshall's real estate office as an agent and had quickly made a name for herself. At first, Kelly had enjoyed the times Peggy came for dinner because the house resounded with laughter and her dad was happier than she had seen him since before her mom became sick. But then she had begun to notice that they spent more and more time together, and she soon resented their closeness and the jokes they shared. After that, Kelly invented reasons to head to her room when Peggy came around, and on weekends she stayed as late as possible at the stables.

Kelly remembered clearly the day, two months ago, that the bomb had been dropped. Her dad had called her and Emily into the family room and with a glowing face had told them that Peggy had agreed to become his wife and their mother. Emily had been thrilled. She had been only seven when her mom died and at age eleven she was ready for a new mother. If her dad saw the horror written all over Kelly's face, he ignored it. She had stiffly given him her congratulations and then escaped to her room where she had sobbed out her misery and frustration. There had already been so much change in her life. She didn't want any more. It was then she had resolved she would never accept the intruder as her new mother.

"Good morning, Kelly!"

Kelly thoughts were interrupted by the greeting, and she braked her bike to a stop in front of Granddaddy Porter. He wasn't really her grandfather, but everyone she knew called the owner of Porter's Stables by that name. She had known Granddaddy for nine years, having started taking lessons at age six.

"Hi, Granddaddy Porter."

Taking his well-worn pipe out of his mouth he said, "You're up awfully early this morning. What's up? I know your dad is marrying that pretty Peggy Landers this afternoon. I imagine you're excited over having a new mom."

Kelly was pretty sure he knew how she *really* felt. Granddaddy Porter always seemed to know what she was really feeling, but in the months since the announcement Kelly had kept her mouth shut, and he had left her to her own thoughts. Now she forced a weak smile. "Yeah, it's a big day. I just thought I'd get up early so I could go for a ride before breakfast and before everyone gets to the house."

The wedding was to be a simple affair held at their home followed by a large reception in their own yard. Between Kelly's dad and Peggy, they knew most of the small town, and people would be in and out all day.

"Well, sure, you can go for a ride. But you take it easy. It's Saturday and these horses have a long day ahead of them. I don't want you doing any wild riding to let out any frustrations you might be feeling." He fixed her with a steady gaze as he talked to her.

Kelly flushed with embarrassment and anger as he spoke. Embarrassment that Granddaddy could know her thoughts so well, and anger that he thought she would mistreat any of the horses she loved so much. "Don't worry, Granddaddy," Kelly quickly assured him. "I'm just going for a short ride, and you should know I won't make any of the horses too tired. In fact, I was thinking about taking Smokey. Only the advanced students can ride him, so he won't have as long a day as the others."

"You go ahead then. Make sure you put him in the back paddock when you're done so he'll have plenty of water and shade while he's waiting for his classes." He started to walk away and then swung back around to remark, "That Mrs. Jacobsen called and was real disappointed you wouldn't be here to teach her two boys today. She thinks you're the best beginner teacher we have ever had here. Says no one else has the patience you do. I told her you would be back to work next week, so she decided to take her boys to the amusement park today and wait for you to return. You're doing a good job, Kelly. I'm real proud of you." He gave her a look warm with affection then turned and walked off.

Kelly knew he was trying to make her feel better. The words *did* fill her with a good feeling. She had started teaching her beginner classes just three months ago, and she worked hard to do a good job. She actually loved working with the young kids who came, so awed by the size of the horses. Mrs. Jacobsen's two boys were her favorites. In addition to the satisfaction she felt, teaching classes also assured her she could ride anytime she wanted. Kelly was trading out her time in exchange for riding privileges and advanced lessons once a week from the stable trainer. She was happy with the arrangement.

Turning toward the barn, she reflected for a minute on how much she loved Porter's. Granddaddy's operation had been here for a long time. All the buildings were weathered and worn, but the place was spotlessly clean and carefully organized to meet Granddaddy's high expectations. The barn seemed to glow in the early morning sun, and the soft sounds of horses munching their morning meal and snuffling comments to each other filled the air. Such sounds were music to Kelly.

Smokey was just finishing his meal when Kelly slipped into his stall. He nickered a soft greeting. Throwing her arms around his neck, she absorbed some of his warmth and solidity. Already she could feel the place working its magic on her. She quickly groomed, then saddled and bridled him. Smokey was an old horse, but he still had a lot of life. Smokey had been on his way to a processing plant when Granddaddy bought him at an auction three years ago. The retired rodeo horse had reminded Granddaddy of a horse he had owned as a boy, so he brought him to the stables, thinking he could live out his days in the big, green pasture.

Instead of going into retirement, though, Smokey had quickly become a favorite at Porter's. He was too much for the less-experienced riders, but the advanced riders competed for the chance to ride him. His rodeo life had given him a tough mouth, so a rider had to be strong to control him. He was full of life and loved to dance around, acting like he was going to give you the ride of your life. Smokey was just what Kelly needed to take her mind off her father's wedding.

Mounting quickly, she reined Smokey into the woods and breathed a sigh of relief as they eased onto the forested trail. Light filtered softly through the tangle of branches, and the air seemed aglow with the softness of spring. The woods were full of flitting birds, and Kelly noticed the white and pink crocus carpeting the ground and the ferns that were just beginning to uncurl from their winter beds.

Smokey demanded her attention as he danced up to the stream. Kelly took a firm grip with her legs, knowing he wouldn't be content to merely walk through it like any other horse. She leaned forward as she felt him gather his body. Lightly they soared over the water, and Kelly let him have his head as he cantered up the trail. After only a few hundred yards she pulled him down to a slow trot. "You, sir, have a lot of work to do today, and you can't use all of your energy acting like a little kid!" Smokey snorted his disgust but let her have her way.

Kelly loved horses with all her heart. She had spent the last eight years living, breathing, and talking horses. While Smokey and the rest of Granddaddy's horses were very special to her, her dream was to have her very own. Kelly spent hours imagining what it would be like. Her horse would be the most beautiful animal alive, and it would do everything better than any other horse. It would respond to the lightest touch and would love to jump as much as she. In her mind Kelly could see them clearing hurdle after hurdle for the sheer fun of it.

Having her own horse meant a lot of work, though. Kelly's father firmly believed that anything worth having is worth working for. He had told Kelly that he would match whatever she earned to buy her horse. For the last year she had spent every possible minute babysitting and doing yard work for their neighbors. Almost every bit of her pay was stashed away in her savings account. Kelly figured that in another year she would have enough to present to her father.

After an hour of wandering through the woods and letting the peace and quiet prepare her for the day ahead, Kelly turned Smokey back to the stable. Realizing she was getting short on time, she hurried through the necessary work. Untacking him, she went over his glistening body with a stiff rubber brush. She loved to watch his lips curl as he delighted in her touch. She followed this with a softer brush and then finished with a soft cloth. Giving him a quick kiss on the nose, she turned him loose in the paddock and headed for her bike.

Seeing Granddaddy on the porch of his weather-beaten house, she gave him a quick wave and pedaled rapidly for home. Her time at the barn had been a welcome respite, but now she would have to face the reality of her father's marriage.

T W O

Well, look who's the early bird this morning! I heard the garage door earlier. I figured you had gone out to Granddaddy's for a ride. Have a good time?" Her father spoke without turning from the stove where he was deftly turning her favorite—blueberry pancakes.

Kelly's heart constricted when she realized that soon Peggy would be joining them for breakfast *every* morning. Slipping up behind her father, she wrapped her arms around his waist and answered, "I sure did. It's a beautiful morning. Getting there so early, I felt like I had the place to myself. You would have loved it." Kelly wanted to add, "Only you never go riding anymore," but she held her tongue. In the past her father had joined her on many of her rides, but in the year since Peggy had invaded their lives, it had become less and less frequent. He was always with *her.*

"I'm sure I would have, honey." Her father gave her a warm smile.

Reaching into the refrigerator for some orange juice, Kelly apologized, "Sorry I didn't get home in

15

time to start breakfast. I thought I'd have plenty of time."

Her father flipped two thick pancakes onto a plate. "This day is too important to laze around in bed. Peggy will be here soon to finish the flower arrangements. Don't you think it was great she wanted to do them herself? She said it'd make it all seem more special." Not giving her time to respond, he hurried on. "After four long years, you and Emily are going to have a mother, and I will have a wife again. I loved your mother dearly and I've missed her more than you can possibly imagine, but I can't help believing that she knows and approves."

The kitchen door banged open, saving Kelly from having to dream up something nice to say in response to her father's speech. Eleven-year-old Emily barreled into the kitchen with an enthusiastic, "Good morning, everybody! Just think! In a few hours the house will be full of wedding guests, and Peggy will become ours for good!"

Her father grinned and teasingly pulled one of Emily's long, blonde braids. People were amazed that Kelly and Emily were sisters. Just as Kelly was the spitting image of their father, Emily was a tiny replica of their mother. Her silky blonde hair framed a heart-shaped face adorned by emerald green eyes. Anyone could see that in a few years she would be a heart stopper. And while Kelly tended to be serious about things, falling into moods that would take her days to come out of, Emily was convinced life was always wonderful, charming people with her happy-go-lucky attitude. Yet for all their differences, they were very close. Their mother's early death had created a deep bond between them.

Emily didn't see the glare that Kelly sent shooting her way. *Peggy has even managed to cause a rift between Emily and me*, she thought angrily. Kelly's bitter resentment of her father's marriage was matched by Emily's enthusiastic approval. Kelly felt betrayed by everyone she loved, reinforcing her decision to *never* accept the intruder who was soon to become her stepmother. She, her dad, and Emily had gotten along just fine for the past four years, and she didn't want anyone or anything changing it!

Kelly finished filling the juice glasses as Emily brought out the syrup and butter. They all slipped into their chairs as her father placed the steaming pancakes on the sturdy oak table. Sunlight streamed through the wide bay window, turning the breakfast nook into a tiny golden palace. When Kelly was younger she had imagined that her father was the king and she and Emily the princesses. Today, all she could think was that Peggy would soon take her place as the unwanted queen.

Picking up her fork, Kelly prepared to dive into the fluffy mass set before her. Her father cleared his throat, halting her fork in midair. "We haven't said the blessing yet, honey," he said quietly.

Stiffly she bowed her head, but her eyes remained open in defiance. Her father's rich voice filled the room. "Lord, thank you for this beautiful spring day. Thank you for the joy of Peggy joining us as mother and wife. We're thankful for all your gifts to us, including this meal. In Jesus' name, Amen."

Emily broke the short silence. "Isn't Peggy supposed to be here soon? She asked me to dig out mom's old crystal vases—said they would be beautiful filled with daisies and mums from the garden. Do you know where they got to?"

As Emily and her father discussed what needed to be done before the guests began to arrive, Kelly dug into her pancakes and brooded over her life. Everything was changing and she wanted it to stay the same! Until six months ago, the blessing had never been asked at their table. The fact that it was now could also be blamed on Peggy. She had talked her father into going to church, and shortly after, the blessing had started. Kelly had also overheard a conversation they had late one evening when they thought she was asleep. She hadn't understood most of it—something about her father being saved and then a lot of stuff about praying and the Bible and going to church. Her father hadn't missed a Sunday since then, and sometimes Emily joined him and Peggy. Thankfully, Kelly wasn't made to go. Sundays were her only free days at the stables without lessons and chores, and she treasured them.

Since that late-night talk she had overheard, she had noticed that her father seemed more relaxed and happier, but Kelly didn't want to have anything to do with a God who would bring all this change into her life. Gulping down the last bite of her pancakes, Kelly shoved her chair back from the table and rose to begin clearing off the table.

"Just a minute, honey," her dad said. "Things are going to get pretty hectic around here soon. I want to make sure that y'all understand everything before the guests begin to arrive. Now..."

"Dad!" Emily rolled her eyes in exasperation. "You've told us at least ten times before! Aunt Bev will be staying with us after you and Peggy take off on your honeymoon, and you'll be back in two weeks. You want us to be good and mind Aunt Bev. If we're good, you'll bring us back some really terrific gifts from the Bahamas. Don't worry. Kelly and I won't mess up getting presents from that place!"

Her dad smiled sheepishly as he glanced fondly at Emily. "I guess you're right, sweetheart. Aunt Bev and you two are good friends. I just don't want anything to go wrong while Peggy and I are gone."

Kelly's thoughts were dark as she headed for her room. *If you were so concerned, you wouldn't be marrying that intruder. And you wouldn't be taking off and leaving us all alone.*

• • •

Kelly took a deep breath and pasted a pleasant smile on her face as the music for the wedding prelude began. She had managed to hide safely in her room the entire morning, but Aunt Bev had called her down to join the wedding party as soon as she had arrived. It helped to have Aunt Bev by her side. She was her mother's youngest sister, and they had always been close.

There were less than a dozen people in the room. Only family had been invited to the ceremony. Friends were waiting outside in the beautifully decorated yard for the reception to begin.

On any other occasion Kelly would have been swelling with pride at the sight of her father. Tall and slim, he looked handsome and distinguished in his tailored suit. His wide blue eyes were set off well by his coppery curls and deeply tanned face.

As the opening notes of the wedding march were played, she rose dutifully with the rest to honor the bride. No one looking at her would have guessed the misery that was hidden by her plastic smile. As much as she hated the idea of Peggy invading their lives, she didn't want to cause her father any unhappiness on his wedding day. And even though he didn't care that he was destroying her life, she was determined to suffer alone.

As Peggy floated down the red carpet that had been unrolled just this morning in the sun-filled front room, Kelly grudgingly admitted that she was indeed very pretty. Her simple white dress was lovely against her lightly tanned skin. Her thick, black hair was gently waved to frame her face, and her violet eyes glowed with love and happiness.

While her father and Peggy recited their vows, Kelly ceased her bitter brooding long enough to think with a hint of longing about the days when she and Peggy had laughed and shared town secrets. That was before the wedding announcement. Since that time, Kelly had virtually ignored Peggy and was polite only when her father was in the room to notice. She could accept Peggy as a friend, but she couldn't and wouldn't accept her as her father's wife and her stepmother.

Kelly nursed her feelings of resentment until Aunt Bev motioned for her to rise at the end of the ceremony. She and Emily were to follow their father and new mother down the aisle. Her aunt gave her hand a squeeze and flashed an encouraging smile. Kelly's heart warmed at the gesture. Surely Aunt Bev knew how she felt. She had been her mom's closest sister and had been an unending source of support for them all when her mom had died. At least Kelly would have a two-week reprieve before she had to face life with Peggy as her mother.

• • •

Allowing the warm spring air to soothe her tired body, Kelly leaned back against the windowsill and gazed out on the night. It had seemed that most of the town had been waiting in the yard after the ceremony. An endless stream of people had commented that Kelly must, of course, be *very* happy for her poor, lonely father, and that she must be just *thrilled* to have lovely Peggy Landers—now Peggy Marshall—as her new mother! Kelly had been hard put not to spew out her resentment. Her poor father, indeed! As far as she was concerned, she, Emily, and her father had been doing just fine. True, she had missed her mother, but they had managed.

Hours of forcing her pleasant smile had left Kelly exhausted. As soon as the crowd had waved her father and Peggy off on their honeymoon, she had escaped to her room. After the last guest had departed, Aunt Bev had come looking for her, but Kelly had pretended to be sound asleep on her bed. After giving her a kiss on the cheek, Aunt Bev had slipped back downstairs.

Sitting at her window, Kelly munched the sandwich that her aunt had left by the bed. She was glad Aunt Bev had been able to come. Her dad and Peggy had talked about bringing in a sitter from the agency in town, but at the last minute Aunt Bev had rear-ranged her schedule so she could be there.

Staring through the arms of the old oak sentinel guarding her window, Kelly was comforted by the gleam of the few stars that could penetrate the leafy canopy. After the flurry of today's activities, she welcomed the comforting silence that enveloped the town. Unbidden, Kelly's thoughts traveled back to the times her mother had joined her on the win-dowsill. Before she crawled into bed, she and her mother would talk softly about the events of the day, and her mother would answer the serious questions of her young life. Wrapped in her mother's love, Kelly had always fallen asleep as soon as her head touched the pillow.

After her mother's death, she had contented her-self with memories. Her mother was gone, but the house was still full of her warmth and presence. There was no room for Peggy. Her father might have a new wife and Emily might be thrilled about her new mother but she, Kelly, would never accept her. And she would certainly never accept this new religion her father had gotten involved in.

With that last defiant thought, Kelly crawled into bed and cried herself to sleep.

THREE

At eleven o'clock in the morning it was already hot. The weatherman had said the night before that North Carolina was experiencing an unusually warm spring. Kelly believed him as she wiped the sweat off her forehead with the red bandanna that was always handy when she taught.

Crossing her arms over the weathered wooden fence, she gazed around the stables that she loved so much. It was Saturday again, and the place was bursting with activity. Classes were going in all four rings, and the chatter of children and adults mingled with the shouted instructions of teachers. The thud of countless horse hooves hitting the hard ground completed the harmony. Granddaddy was propped back in his old, cane rocking chair, entertaining the students' parents with stories of his childhood days on a Western ranch. Kelly knew most of them were wildly exaggerated, but the people enjoyed hearing them and Granddaddy certainly enjoyed telling them. On this beautiful day no one really cared what was fact or fiction. It was enough to be a part of this

wonderful spring unfolding under a perfect Carolina sky.

Kelly had one more beginner class to teach before
she was done for the day. Even though she was hot,
she was looking forward to the next class. She always
finished out the morning with the two Jacobsen
boys. They were her favorites.

Her two-week reprieve was almost up. Her dad
and Peggy would be home tomorrow afternoon.
They had called several times during their honeymoon, but Kelly had always managed to make herself scarce so she wouldn't have to talk to them. She
had missed her father but having Aunt Bev had
been great fun. And she was glad not to have to deal
with the problem of Peggy for a while. She and her
aunt had shared some good talks, but whenever
Aunt Bev brought up the topic of Peggy, Kelly had
swiftly changed the subject. She was sure her aunt
guessed her resentment, but Aunt Bev hadn't pushed
and Kelly was grateful.

Kelly's thoughts were brought back to the task at
hand when the Jacobsen boys—Chuck, ten, and
Frank, eight—piled out of their pickup shouting
her name.

"Hi, guys! Hello, Mrs. Jacobsen!" She flashed her
even, white smile. "Today's the big day for Chuck
and Frank. If they pass my test, they'll be able to
move on to the intermediate class. I'll miss 'em, but
they've worked hard and I think they're ready for
it."

"You better believe they're excited!" Mrs. Jacobsen's eyes sparkled with amusement. "I could hardly
get them to eat this morning. All they could talk

about was getting out of the 'baby ring' and into the 'big ring.'"

Kelly pretended to be hurt. "Well, gosh, guys. I thought you liked me, and here you can hardly wait to get rid of me."

Undaunted, they gave her big grins. "Aw, you know we like you," Chuck said. "But you're not going anywhere. We're ready to do more than just poke around the ring at a trot."

Kelly laughed. "I can remember a time not too long ago when you were scared to death to do more than walk. But you're right. Y'all are ready for the big time if I don't miss my guess. Let's go."

After the boys were mounted and were at attention in the middle of the ring, Kelly began. "Okay guys, here's what I'm looking for. We've spent the last four months learning balance, the importance of good hands, how to both post and sit the trot, not to mention the rules of horsemanship and safety. First, we'll have the riding portion of the test, and then I'll test you verbally. Chuck, I want you to go first. Go ahead and move Dixie out onto the rail."

With a light squeeze of his legs, Chuck took a firm grip on the reins and eased the sturdy pinto pony out where Kelly had indicated. "Go around once at a walk, and then I want you to do a posting trot on the outside diagonal. Remember to keep your hands low and your heels down."

His face tight with concentration, Chuck moved Dixie into a trot as he came level with Kelly the second time around. He was very careful not to kick Dixie, but just to squeeze the mare tighter with his legs to make her trot. Rising smoothly to the steady one-two beat, Chuck circled the ring at a posting trot. Glancing down to check his diagonal, he sat through one of the beats. When he resumed posting, he was on the correct diagonal.

Kelly spoke without taking her attention from Chuck. "Frank, why is it important for Chuck to be on the correct diagonal?"

Frank thought before he answered. "When he posts to the outside front leg," he finally said, "Dixie's inside back leg takes all of Chuck's weight when he sits. Since her back leg doesn't have as far to go in the circle, it makes it easier for her."

Kelly flashed him an approving glance and spoke warmly, "That's exactly right! I couldn't have said it better myself." Turning her attention back to Chuck, she watched him carefully. He was sitting straight and tall in the saddle and his heels were down—most of the time. Focusing on his hands, Kelly was pleased to see that he held the reins firmly in both hands and maintained light contact with Dixie's mouth. He wasn't using the reins to balance himself as most beginner riders seemed to do. Turning out students with "good hands" was important to her, and she let no one advance who had not mastered that art. She didn't think it was fair to punish a horse's mouth just because a rider hadn't learned how to use his legs and balance to stay on.

"Let's see a complete circle at the end of the ring, Chuck." Taking a firmer grip with his legs, Chuck moved his inside leg slightly behind the girth in order to push Dixie's hindquarters around. At the same time he pulled slightly on the inside rein, and together they smoothly completed the turn.

"Bring her on in now, Chuck. You did an excellent job! You still need to work some on keeping your heels down, but that will come with practice." His face flushed with pleasure at her praise. "Now Frank, it's your turn. Do you think you can repeat what Chuck just did?"

Concentrating too hard to answer, Frank merely nodded his head. His freckled face was puckered with thought and his blue eyes were deadly serious.

Kelly smiled. "Hey, guy! Relax some. This isn't the firing squad—it's a simple riding test. You're going to do fine." A smile flitted across Frank's face, but he didn't answer in response to Kelly.

Ten minutes later Kelly called him in. "You did a great job, Frank. I wish all of my students had the natural balance and seat that you two have. If you can do as well on the verbal part as you did on the riding, I guess I'll have to get rid of you two."

Chuck and Frank exchanged looks of delight at the victory they saw within their reach. They knew they had done their homework.

"Frank, tell me two of the rules of horsemanship that we've talked about in the last four months."

Relaxed in the saddle now that the riding test was over, Frank replied with confidence. "Well, one of the most important ones is to always respect your horse, that way he'll respect you. Try to understand why he acts the way he does because there is always a reason. Another would be to never take chances with a strange horse. I know Snowball here pretty well and know what to expect from her." He patted her affectionately on her thick, white neck. "But I need to always be thinking around strange horses, and I need to move slowly and carefully so I don't scare them."

Kelly nodded her approval and then turned to Chuck. "Can you give me two more?"

"I know that I should always be nice to other riders," Chuck replied. "Whenever I finally get out of this ring, I know not to ride on the heels of other horses. And I need to watch for a horse that has his ears laid back. He might be getting ready to bite or kick." Kelly nodded her approval and he continued, "Another would be never to give a hot horse all the water he wants. It might make him sick. You need to walk him and give him just a little bit of water every little while until he is cool and has had all he wants. Of course, until I get out of here, I'll never have the chance to ride a horse enough to get him hot and put the rule into practice!"

"Okay, wise guy," Kelly laughingly said. "If you can name two of the safety rules, then maybe you'll get your chance."

"Let's see," Chuck took a moment to think. "Never go near strange horses until you are sure it is safe, and never use the reins to tie your horse. That's a good way to end up with a broken bridle. Always keep a rope and halter around and use that." Chuck smiled triumphantly as he finished.

Frank repeated his brother's perfect performance, and Kelly faked a heavy sigh. "Well, I guess I'm about to lose my favorite students." Smiling quickly, she congratulated them. "You both did a fine job. I know I'll hear good reports from your next classes. You both will turn out to be fine horsemen if you keep working so hard. Make sure you come by and say hi when you're here. In the meantime, let's go meet your new teacher."

Frank and Chuck whooped with joy and followed her from the ring.

"Mandy, I have some new students for you. They are more than ready for your intermediate class. Chuck and Frank are already good riders." Kelly spoke with pride to the stable trainer. Not only was Mandy Kelly's own teacher, but she was also a good friend.

"I know if you say they're ready, they are." Mandy smiled at the boys. "It's great to have a beginner teacher who does such a good job. It makes my job a lot easier."

Kelly flushed with pleasure at Mandy's words, gave both of the boys a hug, and headed for lunch.

• • •

Syringe in hand, Kelly murmured soothingly as she approached Brandy. "Easy boy, this will only last a second and then it'll be over. You don't want to take a chance on getting sick like some of your friends, do you?" Moving smoothly up to the side of his head, she waited patiently until Mandy had a good hold of his halter. "Okay, my friend. Relax that stiff neck some—there! It's all over." Kelly slid the needle back out and gave him a loving pat. Brandy stopped quivering and gradually his eyes stopped rolling. She murmured to him for another minute and slipped out of his stall.

Kelly was grateful to have the opportunity to learn a new skill in horse care, but she regretted the situation that had caused it. Just last week Granddaddy had bought a new class horse from a local horse trader. Everyone had been thrilled because Tony, the new addition, had gaits smooth as glass and was a joy to ride. After only two days, though, he had become sick and developed a runny nose and terrible cough. The vet had diagnosed a severe cold. Tony had been immediately separated from the rest of the horses, but the damage was already done. Within the week several of the horses had started coughing. Granddaddy had ordered the shots of penicillin to combat the infection in the other horses— both his and the ones that were boarded there. Brandy was the last horse to be given the shot, and after forty horses, Kelly felt like a pro.

"Whew! I sure hope that takes care of 'em all," she said to Mandy. "What a bum thing to happen to Granddaddy. That dumb horse trader! What if all the horses get sick? How will we have classes?"

Granddaddy had walked quietly up behind her while she was talking and laid a hand on her shoulder. "I think we caught it in time, Kelly," he said. "My horses are healthy. It was just the fairly new ones that caught Tony's cold. And don't blame the horse trader. I've been doing business with Ron for years. He's never brought me anything but fine horses. He had just picked Tony up and had no way of knowing he was sick." Putting an arm around Kelly, he smiled warmly. "You did a fine job giving the shots. Mandy said she only had to show you a few times before you took it over. You're learning fast. If you keep it up, I'll have to turn the stables over to your care."

"And put me out of a job?" Mandy laughed good-naturedly as she left the stables and headed toward the ring.

But Kelly remained serious.

"Granddaddy, I want to learn everything I can. Someday when I have my own horse, I want to take as good care of it as you take of yours. Everyone says you have the best horses in Kingsport."

"You keep sticking around Mandy and you'll soon know everything you need to take care of your own horse. She's the best trainer in all of North Carolina, as far as I'm concerned, and she is real impressed with your ability." He turned to leave, but stopped. "By the way, aren't your father and your pretty new mother coming home tomorrow?"

The glow of Granddaddy's words dimmed at the mention of her stepmother. "What? Oh, yeah. Dad and Peggy should get in after lunch tomorrow. I'm supposed to be there, so I won't be able to be here for the whole day. I'll be out early and stay as long as I can." Not wanting to answer any more questions about Peggy, Kelly edged away. "See you later. I've got more work to do before my jumping lesson."

She couldn't help hearing his last words. "Peggy is a good woman, Kelly. Give her a chance. You might find yourself liking the chance to have a new mother. At your age you need one."

Ferociously, she attacked the stalls she had to clean. *Peggy is a good woman, Kelly.* Who cared if Peggy was a good woman? Certainly not she! Good woman or not, she was nothing but an intruder in their home. And all that mess about needing a mother. She and Emily had gotten along fine with just their father.

Slowing her furious pace, Kelly laughed ruefully at herself. At this rate she wouldn't have the energy to finish the rest of her stalls. Pushing thoughts of Peggy out of her mind, she concentrated on her work. Kelly was now in the boarders' section of the barn. She had an arrangement with five of the local townspeople to clean their horses' stalls three times a week. She had grabbed the opportunity. Every bit of money she could stash away would bring her that much closer to having her own horse. Working swiftly but carefully, she allowed her thoughts to wander...

Cantering down the wooded trail, she and Crystal check their speed as they come up on a fallen log. Kelly leans forward as Crystal gathers her body and with a triumphant leap they sail over the obstacle. It is only one in a series of jumps that are all handled with the same ease. Coming to a halt in front of the cheering people, Kelly reaches down to reward Crystal with a pat. Tall, black, and shiny, Crystal tosses her head at the people, as if they are her subjects. Barely breathing hard after their wild run, she turns her head to nudge Kelly's foot as if to say, "I love you."

Voices in the barn broke into her dream. Putting all her attention into her chores, Kelly finished quickly. Carefully putting away the shovel and rake, she hurried to the main barn. Seeing that Mandy was still busy with some of her students, Kelly ducked into the clubhouse and downed almost a quart of cold water. Her work had built up an incredible thirst. Allowing her body the luxury of a few minutes' rest, she smiled in memory of her dream in the stall. In her mind she had already named her dream horse Crystal, and she would be tall, black, and shiny. Now if Kelly could just *find* such an animal. Most of the horses around Kingsport were various shades of brown and gray, and she had yet to see a solid black horse such as the one she dreamed about.

Mandy was waving goodbye to her last student when Kelly emerged from the coolness of the club-house. Hurrying into the barn, Kelly saddled and bridled Jackson, the tall bay she would be using for her jumping lesson this week. Leading him into the bright sunlight, she caught herself wishing that Mandy had assigned her another horse. Jackson was an excellent jumper but only when he felt like it. There were days when he obviously felt that jump-ing was beneath his dignity. On those days it took all the skill Kelly had to urge him over the obstacles.

Mandy caught the look on her face and accurately interpreted it. "I know Jackson can be a real hard-head. But if you can learn how to handle horses like him, then you're well on your way to being a horse-woman. It'll take skill and experience to train the horse you'll own one day."

"I know, Mandy. I'm just a little tired, that's all. Who knows? Maybe this will be a day Jackson enjoys the thought of being a jumper."

Kelly's prediction turned out to be true, and the next hour was a joy. There was nothing Kelly enjoyed more than sailing over the obstacles in the jump course that Mandy had designed for her advanced students. Following Mandy's instructions, Kelly worked Jackson through lead changes, figure eights, and both trotting and cantering over the course. The jump course included several in-and-outs, two stone walls, and Mandy had even had one of Grand-daddy's hired hands dig a trench for a water jump. Jackson's stubbornness had landed Kelly in the water more than once, but today he soared over the water as if it weren't there.

Her face flushed with happiness and exertion, she reined Jackson into the center of the ring when Mandy called her in after the lesson. "You improve every week. I would hate to lose such a good beginner teacher, but I may have to move you up to the intermediates soon."

Kelly smiled happily at Mandy's praise but didn't quite know what to say. Her goal was to be as good as Mandy Chapman someday. It thrilled Kelly to have her hero's approval.

"You've worked hard today, and I know Jackson's not tired. Why don't you head for the woods and enjoy the next hour? You can feed him when you get back in and then turn him out with the rest of the horses."

"Thanks, Mandy!" Kelly enthusiastically responded. "And if you want, you can sleep in tomorrow morning. I'm planning on coming out real early since my dad's coming home, so I'll be here in time to feed the horses. I know you don't have many mornings to sleep late, and I really enjoy feeding them."

"That would be great! You've made me an offer I can't refuse. Why don't you come on over to my trailer about ten o'clock, and I'll have breakfast ready for you. How's that for a deal?"

Kelly grinned. "Ask my dad. He'll tell you I *never* turn down food. See you tomorrow morning."

The next hour was just what Kelly needed. She and Jackson meandered slowly down the darkening trails. She was free to dream to her heart's content about Crystal. The peace of the wooded sanctuary slowly worked its magic on her. As she emerged from the woods and headed for the barn, she felt ready to face her dad and Peggy tomorrow. Whistling, she turned Jackson loose after his supper and headed her bike toward home.

FOUR

An explosive sigh burst from Kelly as she reined Smokey through the maze of fallen logs. It had been another hot, long Saturday at the stables. Even though she loved every moment of her life there, she had to admit she was bone-tired. Dad and Peggy had been home one full week, and it had been every bit as hard as she had known it would be. She tried to be polite—she even sickened herself sometimes with her sweetness—that is, when she could find no way to avoid encounters with her stepmother.

The whole week she had managed to be late getting ready for school so that she had only to mumble a greeting as she dashed out the door. Her mornings at school had been interrupted by her growling stomach, but at least she hadn't been forced to endure another meal with that woman. Accustomed to dashing home after school, she now hung around talking to all her friends. When she did arrive home, it was just in time to dash off to either the stables or her after-school jobs. In order to escape her father's certain wrath, though, she was forced to eat dinner with the rest of the family. But she never spoke unless she was asked a direct question, and then, if possible, she answered only with a yes or no. She even bowed her head during the blessing, but she refused to close her eyes and she most certainly was not praying. As soon as dessert had been served, she used homework as an excuse to flee to her bedroom where she would stay for the remainder of the night.

"Easy now, boy!" Smokey demanded Kelly's full attention as he shied away from a piece of flying paper. Head erect and ears pointed sharply forward, he pranced sideways down the trail. Snorting nervously, he refused to calm down under her soothing touch. Jolted out of her thoughts, Kelly became abruptly aware that the weather had undergone a dramatic change in the thirty minutes since she had entered the woods.

The sun that had blazed down on her all day as she taught was now tucked firmly behind a massive dark cloud. The wind had increased to a frightening intensity, causing the trees around her to bend and sway. The air was beginning to fill with flying debris. The sky, which had been so light and fragrant with spring just minutes earlier, now seemed to thicken with the threat of a late March thunderstorm.

Realizing how dangerous it would be if she were caught in the woods in a violent storm, Kelly whirled Smokey around and headed for the barn. She could blame only herself if she or Smokey were hurt. Preoccupied with her bitter thoughts, she had paid no attention to the approaching storm. Allowing Smokey to break into a canter, she still maintained a tight hold on the reins. It would be just as dangerous to allow him to panic and run out of control in the swiftly darkening woods. Her heart in her mouth, Kelly carefully reined him around fallen logs and calmed him with her voice every time he jumped at falling limbs and flying debris.

After what seemed an eternity, they emerged from the woods across from the stables. Kelly could see Mandy and Granddaddy standing in the open doorway.

"Run for it!" they shouted in unison.

Giving Smokey his head, Kelly dashed across the open field and ducked into the barn door just as the sky split with a resounding crash. Torrents of rain began to fall as Kelly slid off the steaming horse's back.

"What in the world were you doing out there, Kelly? Don't you know you could have been killed? And look at Smokey—he's so hot he's steaming. My gosh, girl, have you lost your senses?"

"Granddaddy, I'm so sorry!" Kelly tried hard to control the tears she knew were about to flow. "It's all my fault. I was thinking and not paying any attention to what was going on. By the time Smokey warned me about the storm, it was too late to do anything but run to escape it! I promise not to leave until he's completely cool. I'll stay here with him and make sure he has food and water before I turn him out."

Mandy caught the exhausted girl in her arms. "Now both of you calm down. Kelly, you made it back in time and Smokey will cool down just fine. The important thing is that you're safe. Granddaddy was just worried about you."

Turning to the older man, Mandy laughingly challenged him, "Granddaddy, I'm sure there were times when you were young that you did foolish things without thinking."

Kelly smiled at Mandy gratefully as Granddaddy headed into the feed room. His face was still creased with worry, but he allowed a rueful smile as he turned away. "Humph. It wasn't only when I was young that I did foolish things. Kelly, you just be more careful from now on. I'd hate to have to explain to your father how you got hurt while in my care."

• • •

It was after dark when Mandy stopped the stables' pickup truck in front of Kelly's house.

"Thanks for the ride, Mandy," Kelly said as she got out. "It took me longer than I thought to take care of Smokey. Dad would have had a real fit if I had ridden my bike home in the dark."

"Anytime, Kelly. See you in the morning."

Having stowed her bike in the garage, Kelly headed for the house. She hoped everyone had already eaten dinner. She was just too tired to cope with her stepmother. Her exhaustion might make her say something she would mean but possibly regret later.

Pushing the back door open, she realized with dismay that supper was just going on the table. The fragrance of fried chicken, mashed potatoes, and fried okra hit her in the face as she stepped into the room. Her dad caught her up in a big hug as she entered the room.

"Welcome home, my little horsewoman! Grand-daddy called and told us of your narrow escape.

That was some storm. One of the limbs came off the big oak outside and barely missed hitting the house. I'm glad you're still in one piece."

Kelly felt a warm rush of love for her father. Eager words tumbled to her lips but were stilled when Peggy's voice broke into the moment. "We're so glad you're safe. I know fried chicken and okra are your favorite foods, so I put away the spaghetti I had fixed earlier and prepared this special just for you."

Kelly gave her a weak smile despite the bitterness she felt at Peggy's interruption. She knew she should be thankful for what Peggy had done—her father's stern gaze convinced her of that. He was waiting for her to speak.

"Oh, thanks." The words she had intended for her father would remain unsaid. Stifling a deep sigh, she turned to the sink to wash her hands.

As the food passed from hand to hand, Kelly grudgingly admitted that at least they were eating better since Peggy had arrived. Not that she had been unhappy with what they had before. Her dad was a good cook on the few things he knew how to fix, but grilled cheese sandwiches, pork 'n' beans, and hamburgers could get old. She would give up their improved menu gladly, though, if it meant things would go back to being the same.

"Kelly, Peggy took me shopping and bought me a new dress today." Emily's chattering broke into Kelly's thoughts. "It's *beeyootiful!* You should see it—red with a white sash. She even got me some white shoes to match. I'm going to wear it to church tomorrow. Why don't you wear your red one and then we can match!"

"No thanks, Em," Kelly replied. "I won't be going to church. I'm heading out to the barn first thing in the morning."

"But Kelly, Dad said we both had to..." Emily broke off at her father's warning glance. Kelly turned to gaze at her father as he cleared his throat.

"Kelly, we would like you to join us for church in the morning. I know you're not used to going, but I think you will enjoy this church. The pastor is young, and everyone is real friendly."

"I don't think so, Dad. I've made plans to go riding early with Mandy in the morning, and then I'm going to do some work on my own in the rings. Maybe some other time."

"Honey, I know you're used to spending your Sunday mornings at the barn, but Peggy and I have decided that from now on we will all attend church as a family. After lunch, you can spend the rest of the day at the barn."

Kelly dropped her chicken and stared at her father. "You mean you're *making* me go?"

Her father took a deep breath before answering. "Kelly, I know we've never attended church much in the past, but that is going to change. I'm just learning how really important it is. I'm seeing, too, how important it is for you to be there. I had decided this before the wedding, but Peggy and I agreed to wait on going as a family until we got back."

"How thoughtful of you." The sarcastic words were out before she could stop them.

Ignoring her words, her father continued. "I think you'll like this church, Kelly. There are a lot of kids your age there, and I'm told their youth group does a lot of fun things. It will be good for you to get involved in a group like that."

Kelly knew she was treading on dangerous ground, but she couldn't stop the rush of words. "I don't want to be involved in some stupid youth group that is good for me. I want to be out at the stables. Why should I spend Sunday mornings in some stuffy old church when I could be out with the horses doing what I love? Just because you've gone and gotten religion doesn't mean that I have to!"

"Honey, I know you're upset, but Peggy and I have decided we'll all go as a family and that's final."

Kelly knew she should drop it there. Maybe it was the combination of being tired and having had a close call in the woods on top of the week of hidden resentment that made her lose control. "*Peggy and I, Peggy and I.* That's all I hear around here anymore. Nothing is the same since she invaded our lives. Not only do I have to live in the same house with her, but now I'm forced to go to her church. Doesn't anybody care what *I* think, how *I* feel? I wish we could go back to the way things were before I ever heard of someone named Peggy!"

She stopped for a breath and then gave a sharp cry as her father grabbed her arm. "Young lady, you will apologize to Peggy right now. Plenty of people around here care how you feel, if you would get off your high horse long enough to see it. Now apologize!"

Peggy's troubled voice broke in, "Scott, it's okay. Kelly has been through a lot and she's upset. It will take time for all of us to adjust to the changes. Why don't we all just finish our dinner?"

Kelly was beyond caring what she said now. Her voice rose to a fever pitch. "Peggy, I don't need you—especially you—to take up for me. If it weren't for you, none of this would be happening. You've taken my father away from me, you've ruined my home, and now you want to take away the only thing I have left—my time at the stables. Why don't you just leave me alone?" Shoving back her chair, she rushed from the room.

"Kelly!" Her father's booming voice failed to stop her.

"Let her go, Scott." Peggy's voice was quiet. "She's too upset to talk to now. I'm okay. I knew it would be hard." Giving a nervous laugh, she admitted shakily, "I didn't think it would be this hard, but we've given it to God and we'll just have to give him time to work. Getting angry at her won't help any. It will just make things worse."

Emily's small voice broke into the silence that followed. "Does all that mean we won't be going to church tomorrow, that I won't get to wear my new dress?"

Reaching down, Peggy gave the little girl a quick hug. Staring toward the door where Kelly had disappeared moments before, Emily's father answered her in a frustrated voice. "No, Emily—*all* of us are going to church tomorrow. And you'll most certainly get to wear your new red dress."

• • •

Having cried herself to a point of exhaustion, Kelly crept to her windowsill after the house was dark. The storm had passed over, and the sky was brilliant with sparkling stars. Tonight, though, the beauty of the evening and the fragrance of the rain-cleansed air failed to soothe her. The memory of the bitter words still burned in her mind. Her misery was too deep for words. Thoughts of running away filled her mind, but she dismissed them because she really had nowhere to go. How could she possibly face her father tomorrow? She had meant everything she said, but she was sorry she had made her dad angry.

Staring out into the night, Kelly was aware of hunger pangs. She had only taken a few bites of dinner before the battle erupted, and lunch had been skimpy. Listening carefully to be sure no one else was up in the house, Kelly quietly opened her door so she could creep down into the kitchen. Looking down, she gasped in surprise. Placed carefully at the door to her room was a tightly wrapped plate of fried chicken, fruit, and cheese. Could her dad have ... ?

Pulling back into her room, she turned on the little bedside lamp and read the short note: "Kelly, I think I understand. Love, Peggy." Crushing it in her hand, she tossed it in the wastebasket. Her hunger was too great to allow the food to follow it, though. Pushing down her resentment at yet another of Peggy's intrusions, she hastily devoured the food.

FIVE

Being angry with her will do no good, Scott. Try to act like nothing happened last night. After all, she *is* going to church with us."

Kelly's dad gave Peggy an admiring, if somewhat skeptical, smile. "Whatever you say. You're really the one who should be angry, so if you're willing to let it go, then I guess I will too."

Glancing at his watch he yelled up the stairs. "Come on, you two. If you don't get a move on, we'll be late!"

Emily bounced into the room. Moments later they could hear Kelly descending the stairs at a much slower pace.

"Daddy, Daddy, don't you just love my *beeyootiful* red dress? Don't you think I look just *beeyootiful* in it?"

Her father laughed as he swung his youngest daughter into his arms. "You'll be the prettiest girl there, Emily. I'm proud to be your escort, my lady."

Emily was giggling as Kelly entered the room. Swinging Emily back down to the ground, Kelly's father gave the nervous girl a warm look. "Good

47

morning, Kelly. You look very nice in that blue dress. It matches the color of your eyes. Are you ready to go?"

Nodding her head, Kelly could only stare at her father. Was that all he had to say? Nothing more about all the terrible things she said last night? She could hardly believe she would be let off that easy. Surely he was going to punish her or something! The father she knew would have at least told her what a brat she had been before he forgave her. Was this what religion did to people? Shaking her head in wonderment, she caught the smile that Peggy sent her father. So that was it. Peggy had gotten her off the hook. She didn't know how or why, but she wasn't going to tempt fate by asking.

• • •

Having been guided to her Sunday school class by a greeter in the parking lot, Kelly approached the door shyly. She had not been to a church since she was eight years old. Her mother had taken them when Kelly was younger, but after she had gotten sick that had stopped. All Kelly remembered of Sunday school at the other church were the juice breaks and the cookies given to keep them quiet. She had no idea what to expect. Would everyone be serious? Would they spend the whole time praying, and discussing hell and dying? Taking a deep breath, she pulled the door to the classroom open.

"Hello there! Welcome to the senior high class." Kelly felt her hand being grasped warmly by a young man whom she guessed to be in his late twenties. "My name is Martin Stokes, and this is my wife, Janie."

A very attractive lady gave her a warm smile. Kelly smiled back. "Uh, hello. My name is Kelly Marshall."

"Good to meet you, Kelly." Martin smiled.

"Hi, Kelly!" To Kelly's surprise, Julie, her biology lab partner, came walking up. "Are you coming to church here now?"

"Well, sort of." Kelly wasn't exactly sure what to say. She looked around the room in amazement. She saw Erin from her French class, Steve from the football team, and Mike, who played the trumpet in the school band.

"Come and sit by me." Julie led her to a seat near the front.

Kelly had no idea so many of her friends went to church. She wondered if their parents made them go, too. Suddenly, she caught the eye of the new boy who had arrived at school just a few weeks before. He was regarding her with obvious interest, so she flashed him a smile. He rewarded her with a quick grin, then returned his attention to Martin, who was speaking.

"It looks like some of you know our newest arrival, but that's no reason to let her out of the newcomer's tradition! Kelly, before we get started, we'd love to know something about you—how old you are, where you're in school, what you like to do, that kind of thing."

Kelly reddened in embarrassment as all thirty-five people in the room turned their eyes toward her. The thought of talking to the entire class tied her tongue into a hundred knots. Glancing around the room in panic, she caught the eye of the new boy. He gave her a reassuring grin. Kelly summoned all of her courage and stood beside her seat. "My name's Kelly Marshall. I'm fifteen years old, and I'm a sophomore at Kingsport High. Some of you I know from classes. I probably should know others of you, but I usually don't hang around school much at the end of the day. I love horses, and I'm either out at Porter's Riding Stables or I'm working to earn money to buy my own horse." At the thought of missing her usual Sunday fun at the barn, she blurted out before she stopped to think, "I'm not much on Sunday school and church, and I'm only here because my father is making me come."

Kelly turned even redder when she realized what she had said and quickly collapsed into her seat. Several of the kids in the room laughed out loud, which only caused her to feel worse. They would think she was an idiot!

Martin tried to ease her discomfort. In a laughing voice he said, "I imagine a lot of us, if we were as honest as Kelly, would admit we only come to Sunday school because we have to. Janie and I hope to change your minds about it and show you how much fun we can have, and also show you what a good friend Jesus can be. Kelly, welcome to our group."

Kelly was grateful for his words, but still kept her eyes glued to the Bible that was in her lap. Peggy had handed it to her on the way out to the car, but she had no intention of opening it. As Martin's voice continued to flow through the room, she finally allowed her eyes to come up. She realized she was under the scrutiny of the new boy. He gave her another warm smile, and she looked back down. Who was he? Why was he so interested in her? Maybe he was just nice to everyone.

Kelly tried to remember if she knew anything about him. She was pretty sure he was a sophomore at her high school, and she remembered someone saying he had moved here from Texas. She didn't remember having ever heard his name, though. One thing was certain. He was one of the best-looking guys she had seen in a long time. His arms and face were deeply tanned, as if he spent a lot of time outdoors. His dark wavy hair was cut short, and his eyes were as startlingly blue as hers. He was tall and lean, and his smile—it was definitely something else!

Her thoughts broke off as his deep voice filled the room. Kelly had not been paying attention to a word Martin said, but he had obviously asked the new boy from Texas a question. Kelly turned her attention to him as he spoke.

"I think knowing Jesus means everything to me. He's pretty much my best friend. I can tell him anything, and he helped me out a lot when I had to move from Texas and leave all of my friends. I can't imagine not knowing him."

"Thanks, Greg. Anybody else care to share how they feel?"

Several people in the room raised their hands, but Kelly was no longer listening. She had an answer to one of her questions. His name was Greg. It suited him well. But all that stuff about Jesus! She couldn't believe he was caught up in all that religious stuff, too. He looked too smart for that. Did he really mean it when he said Jesus was his best friend? Kelly decided Greg was cute enough for her to forget all that Jesus stuff if he wanted to get to know her better. She wouldn't let it stand in the way of being his friend.

Her thoughts were interrupted again as everyone bowed their heads to pray. She quickly followed their example but still refused to close her eyes.

After Martin said amen, he cleared his throat. "Well, I have what some of you might consider exciting news. Camp Sonshine is ready to do its hiring for the summer season. For those of you who don't know, Camp Sonshine is a Christian camp a few hours from here in the North Carolina mountains. They operate every summer for ten weeks and have over a hundred kids a week there. The campers range in age from six to twelve. Every spring they contact local churches and accept applications from senior high students who have a desire to be either junior counselors or horse wranglers. It's a lot of fun, and the pay is $600 for the summer. Any of you who are interested can see me after class for an application."

Kelly let her breath out slowly as Martin finished speaking. Ten weeks as a wrangler at a camp. And for $600! She could buy her horse *and* she wouldn't have to live with Peggy for all that time. She just had to get that job! Dimly she realized that the class was breaking up, and she responded absently as people spoke to her.

"I'm glad you were here, Kelly. Hope you'll come back."

"Oh, uh yeah, Julie. It was good to see you, too. I'll probably be back. Listen, I'll see you later. I've got to talk to Martin about Camp Sonshine."

Weaving her way through the group, she realized that Greg was already talking with Martin. Catching her eye, Martin broke off what he was saying. "Kelly, I hope you'll be a part of us from now on. Even though your folks are making you come, I want you to feel one of the group."

Kelly flushed at the memory of her earlier remark but managed to smile. "I'm sure you'll be seeing more of me. I wanted to ask you about that wrangler job at the camp. I'd really like to know more."

"That's just what Greg was asking me about. Seems like you two want the same thing. Here are a couple of camp brochures, job descriptions, and applications. Read these and if you have any more questions, I'll try to help you next week. I've got to help get things ready for the service. See y'all later."

As Martin walked away, Greg grinned at Kelly. "You're into horses too, huh? I've noticed you around school, but you always disappeared before I had a chance to talk to you after class. At least now I know where you go. I've heard that Porter's is a pretty nice place. I'm keeping my horse at the Lazy B Stables. It's not as nice a place as Porter's, but it's closer to my house and that means a lot. What do you think about this job? I sure could use the money, and it sounds like fun. Do you have your own horse?"

Kelly laughed and asked teasingly, "Which question do you want me to answer first?"

Greg grinned easily. "I guess I do want to know a lot. Let's head for the church. We can talk on the way. Oh, and you can answer all my questions any way you want."

"Okay. Let's see. Yes, I'm really into horses. I practically live for them. I think this job sounds pretty great. It would be super to get away for the summer, and I could use the money. No, I don't own my own horse yet, but the money from this job would take care of that problem. I'm having to earn a lot of the money for my horse myself, and Camp Sonshine sounds a lot more fun than babysitting and cleaning stalls!"

Kelly and Greg walked slowly over to the church as they talked. She discovered that he had moved from a ranch in East Texas because his folks wanted to be near his father's aging parents who had been sick. Greg had been class president, ridden in a lot of rodeos, and owned a big buckskin gelding named Shandy, who he had raised from a foal born on their ranch five years ago. He also had three little sisters.

Greg discovered that Kelly had lived in Kingsport all her life, had been riding for the past eight years, and taught beginner classes at the local stables. He was impressed by her jumping experience and immediately asked her to teach him how to jump also.

"I'll teach you how to jump, but only if you'll teach me how to ride Western and run the barrels and do other rodeo tricks."

"You're on. That's sounds like a pretty good trade to me. We just have to get the summer job at Camp Sonshine. Who could turn down two people who are so multitalented?" Greg gave her his quick grin again, and Kelly smiled at him happily. Maybe church wouldn't be so bad after all. She felt certain she could endure anything if Greg were around.

As they drew near the church sanctuary, she lowered her voice and asked, "How did you start coming here, anyway? I guess your parents make you come, huh?"

Looking at her in surprise, Greg answered in a firm voice, "Not on your life. Sure my folks come here, too, but I'm here because I want to be. I meant what I said in Sunday school about Jesus being my best friend. I want to know everything I can about him so we can get even closer. Back home we went to a great church, and I was real active in the youth group. I want it to be the same way here." He paused for a moment. "I guess you resent the fact that your parents make you come."

Kelly realized that she might be putting their new friendship in jeopardy, but she felt she had to be honest. She already liked Greg a lot and didn't want to play games with him. "Yes, I resent it. And they're not my parents. At least Peggy isn't. My dad just married her a few weeks ago, and now they are forcing their religion on me. If they want to believe all that Jesus stuff they can, but I don't see why they have to cram it down my throat. Sunday is the day I usually spend at the barn. I don't have any work to do, so I can spend the whole day riding. Now I'm having to spend half of it in a stuffy church."

She caught a glimpse of his troubled face and hastened to add, "I must admit that Sunday school was better than I thought it would be. Martin and Janie seem nice, and it was great to see so many friends there. I'm pretty excited about the prospect of the job, too."

Stopping, she waited for his reaction. Greg's look was one of troubled caring. He hesitated before he spoke. "It's too bad your folks are making you come, but I hope you'll learn to like it. My folks had to make me go to church in Texas until I got to know Jesus. Then I wanted to go on my own. It sounds like you need a best friend, Kelly. I can assure you that Jesus wants to be that." He grew quiet and then added, "I'd really like to be your friend, too."

Kelly had started to grow angry when he was talking about Jesus, because she sure didn't want *him* pushing it on her, but his last quiet words diffused her anger. She knew that she wanted very much to be his friend. Getting angry wouldn't help. "I'd like that, too." There was an awkward pause. "Uh, my dad is waiting now. I'd better go."

"Yeah, I see my folks waiting for me, too. I'll see you around."

S I X

Kelly, who was that good-looking boy you were talking to before church?"

Emily's question burst forth from her mouth before they had even pulled out of the church parking lot. Kelly saw her father and Peggy exchange a glance. She knew they were as interested in her answer as her little sister was. There had been a time when Kelly had eagerly told her father everything about her life, but that had changed. She couldn't stand the thought of him talking about her with Peggy. She pretended to be indifferent about Greg. "Oh, just a guy I know from school."

Emily was clearly disappointed. Kelly knew that with Em's active imagination, she had probably already dreamed up a big romance for her older sister. Not that Kelly hadn't indulged in some of those dreams herself during the church service. It's just that she didn't want to talk about them. There was one thing that she was eager to talk with her father about, though—that summer job at Camp Sonshine!

Her father broke into her thoughts. "I'm really glad you came with us, hon. I hope you had a good time. What did you think of the church?"

She bit off the sarcastic response that came to her lips. Talking to him about the job was too important for her to make him mad. But what was the idea of thanking her for coming? It hadn't been exactly voluntary. He had made her come. She forced a cheerful tone when she answered. "It was all right, Dad. The youth leaders seem like really nice people, and I already know a lot of people in my class."

Her answer obviously relieved him, and they left her alone to her thoughts the rest of the way home. Outside, it had already turned into a beautiful day. Spring had descended on Kingsport in all of its glory. Kelly gazed out at the dogwoods and the riot of daffodils that lined the city's shaded streets. She knew that the woods behind the barn would be alive with the colors of her favorite wildflowers. She had made plans to spend the afternoon on a long trail ride with Mandy. As she gazed out the window, her thoughts drifted to all that had happened that morning.

To be quite honest, she didn't remember anything the pastor had spoken about in church. Her mind had been on Greg. She did remember her surprise that the music was led by a group of casually dressed musicians who played guitars. She had never sung in a church to anything but organ and piano music. In her mind it was a big improvement. Her general impression of the pastor was that he was young and seemed to be nice and easygoing. Other than that, she had paid him no attention. She had been seated where she could view Greg from a side angle and had spent her time dreaming.

Kelly had gone over everything she and Greg had said. She could hardly believe that a boy who was not only fabulous-looking but who also loved horses had been dropped into Kingsport. He had seemed to really like her. She could only hope that she hadn't turned him off with her honesty about going to church. If he really liked her, he wouldn't let a little thing like that bother him. Allowing her thoughts to wander, she dreamed what it would be like to spend a whole summer with him at a camp tucked into the mountains...

• • •

"Kelly, lunch is ready!"

"Coming, Dad." Leaving the brochure and job description scattered on her bed, Kelly bounded down the stairs. She had taken time after changing into her riding clothes to look over the information on Camp Sonshine. She could hardly wait to talk to her dad about it over lunch. He just had to let her apply for the job!

A brief silence followed the blessing as Peggy began to pass the serving dishes around the table. Seeing Emily begin to open her mouth, Kelly broke into the silence before her little sister started to ramble on some silly subject.

"Dad, I want to talk to you about something."

Pausing in his action of heaping potatoes on his plate, he looked at her quizzically. "Go ahead, Kelly."

"Have you ever heard of a place called Camp Sonshine?"

"Why yes, as a matter of fact. Pastor Lou said something about it in the adult Sunday school this morning. Said some of our kids might get to go up there and work for the summer and that the church had been supporting the place for years. Why?"

So far, so good. At least he had *heard* of the place. "The youth leader told us about it this morning and said they were looking for kids to be wranglers. I looked at the brochure before lunch, and the place is just great! I read the job description, too. I know I can do it. They want someone to teach classes, and I already do that. The trail rides will be a piece of cake, and barn chores are nothing new to me. And it pays $600! Dad, I really want to apply for the job." Kelly was breathless when she finished and waited anxiously for his reply.

His face was troubled as he gazed at her. "Kelly, I'm sure you would do a great job, but isn't the job for ten weeks? That's almost the whole summer. I'm not sure that's such a good idea."

"But why, Dad?"

Her father hesitated before he continued. "Honey, I'm just not so sure this summer is such a good time. Peggy just joined us, and we have a lot of adjustments to make as a family. It seems to me that it will take that much longer to get used to the changes if you're gone. Maybe next summer would be better."

Kelly's heart sank at his words, and her thoughts were bitter. So Peggy was even going to ruin her chances of a great summer job. Was this woman going to ruin everything in her life? Struggling to bring her anger under control, she searched desperately for words that would convince her father that he should let her go. Before she could find the right words, though, she heard Peggy's voice break the strained silence.

"Scott, I think Kelly should be allowed to apply for the job," Peggy said. "I went to Camp Sonshine as a child. It's a very special place. I think the experience would be a good one for her. I know this summer may not be the best timing, but it's a chance that would be a shame to miss. I'll still be here when she gets back."

Kelly gaped at her in amazement. Was Peggy actually taking her side? Why in the world would she do a thing like that? Peggy returned her gaze and gave her a gentle smile. Kelly's father cleared his throat, and she swung her attention back to him.

"Well, I guess I'm outnumbered. If Peggy is in agreement, I don't see why you shouldn't give it a try. Honey, I'm sure that if you get the job, you'll be the best wrangler they ever had."

Shoving back her chair, Kelly jumped up and gave her father a big hug. "Oh, Dad, thanks so much. They just have to want me. Being a wrangler at Camp Sonshine would be the perfect way to spend my summer. And just think, with the $600 I could buy my own horse this fall."

Returning her hug, he fixed her with his quiet gaze. "You're welcome, honey. It does sound like a great opportunity. But I'm not the one to thank."

Kelly's eyes fell before his look. He was right, of course. If it hadn't been for Peggy, she wouldn't have even had the chance to apply. Of course she was grateful, but she didn't want to give Peggy the idea that she was accepting her as a mom. Still, she knew her father was waiting for her to say something. "Uh, thanks, Peggy. I appreciate your standing up for me." She allowed Peggy one quick smile and then resumed her seat at the table.

"You're welcome, Kelly. I hope you get the job. And if you want to hear more about Camp Sonshine, just ask me sometime."

"Yeah, okay. Thanks." Kelly knew that Peggy was offering her friendship, but she refused to accept it.

Emily begin to chatter about the happenings at Sunday school, and her father and Peggy turned their attention to her. Kelly was left to her excitement and lofty daydreams of her perfect camp summer—days of endless riding, teaching Greg how to jump (of course, he had to get the job, too!), talking to Greg, working with Greg, free time with Greg...

Her thoughts were interrupted when Emily began to clear the dishes from the table. She watched as Peggy gave her little sister a hug. Why was Peggy so nice all the time? Especially when Kelly was so mean and cold to her? She hadn't said one thing about all the hateful words Kelly had said the night before— just brought her a plate of food in case she got hungry. And then talking her dad into letting her apply for the job!

Well, let her do all the nice things she wanted, Kelly thought to herself. She had vowed never to accept her as a mother, and she intended to keep that vow.

S E V E N

"Hi, Martin. Sorry I'm late." Kelly's face was red as she slid into the chair beside Julie. She hated being late because everyone always looked at you, but this morning couldn't be helped. "My little sister, Emily, spilled milk on her dress right before we walked out the door, and we had to wait for her to change."

Emily had been clowning around in the kitchen and spilled milk on her *beeyootiful* red dress. She had only stopped crying about messing her dress up when their father had promised to take them out for lunch at her favorite restaurant.

"That's okay, Kelly," Martin replied with a smile. "I understand all about little sisters. I was the oldest of nine kids! It's great to see you back again this Sunday. We've got some great things planned that I want you to hear about."

Kelly straightened with a sigh and glanced around the room. Greg was staring at her and flashed her a quick grin. He shrugged his shoulders as if to say he understood about little sisters. He probably did, since he had three. She was thankful to just have one. She was sure that three would drive her crazy! Pulling her eyes away from Greg, Kelly focused her attention on Martin who was talking at the front of the room.

"Last week we talked a little about what it means to have Jesus Christ as a friend. I'd like to focus on that a while longer. I know that to many young people, Christianity is just a bunch of rules and regulations. You know, all the do's and don'ts. *Do* go to church every Sunday, *do* say your prayers every night, *do* honor and respect your parents, etc. But *don't* have too much fun, *don't* drink, *don't* smoke, *don't* use foul language, *don't* mess around too much with the opposite sex. It seems to turn into a battle. The harder your parents and teachers try to make you do and don't, the harder you try to do the don'ts, and don't do the do's!"

Laughter rippled through the room at his play on the words, but everyone, including Kelly, had given Martin their full attention. Kelly, for one, agreed with everything he had just said. Issues between adults and kids did seem to be nothing but a big battle. Who wanted to be a Christian if that's all it meant? She herself was pretty straight—she didn't drink or smoke, and she had never done more than just kiss a guy. Not that she didn't think of more; it just didn't really appeal to her. She didn't want to mess up her life like so many of her other friends. But Kelly figured her friends should lead their own lives the way they wanted. They had enough pressure from their parents without becoming Christians and having the "don't list" get longer.

Martin was speaking again, so Kelly returned her attention to him. "I'm here to tell you that Christianity is more than a set of rules and regulations," he said. "True Christianity is a relationship—a relationship with Jesus Christ. Mankind messed up at the very beginning of history, so God was forced to put a bunch of rules on him. If you want to see a bunch of rules, look at the Old Testament! God planned all along, though, to release his people from that bondage. He didn't want his people to live that way. He created people in the first place to have fellowship with him—to be his friends. Because he wanted their friendship so badly, he decided to send his only son, Jesus Christ, to live with them and then die for them.

"But he didn't stay in the grave. He rose from the dead so we, too, could have life. And not just life, but an abundant life! Now you already know that a true friend is one who chooses to be your friend, willingly and gladly. Not someone you force into it. God knows the same thing, so even after he allowed his only son to suffer and die, he gave us the choice of whether we wanted to accept it or not. If we accept what God did for us through Jesus Christ, then we not only are friends with him, but he also tells us that we will live forever."

Kelly was surprised to find that her hand was gripping her chair so hard that it hurt. She had never before heard the things she was hearing now. This was a far cry from juice and cookies.

"Once you're a true friend of God," Martin continued, "then all those do's and don'ts take on a different meaning. Think of someone who is a true friend. Because you value that friendship, you try not to do things that will hurt that person. You also try to do the things that will make them feel special and happy. You don't do these things because you *have* to. You do them because you *want* to. Well, God wants to be the same kind of friend to you."

Martin glanced around the room and smiled at all the intent faces. "That's enough for one day. We'll talk more about it later. In the meantime, let's talk about the things coming up. Let's see a show of hands of the people who are definitely applying for the jobs at Camp Sonshine."

Kelly raised her hand, along with Greg and two other girls in the room. A shiver of excitement ran through her as she thought of the summer ahead. She just had to get the job! And not only her, but Greg, too! She already knew that the other two girls were applying to be junior counselors. She and Greg were the only ones from their Sunday school applying to be wranglers.

"Great! If any of you need help filling out the application or anything, just let me know. You'll love Camp Sonshine if you get to go. I spent six summers there as a kid, and it was great! Janie, how about if you tell everyone about the cookout we have planned." Martin took the empty chair next to Greg.

Janie launched into her subject with enthusiasm. "Okay, everyone. This is going to be the final event of the school year before people start disappearing for the summer, and we want to make it special. We also want to honor the seniors who are going to be graduating in two months and leaving us."

Everyone laughed as cheers erupted from the bunch of seniors who were almost done at Kingsport High. Kelly knew none of them personally, but she knew all of them by face. Another two years and she would be in their place. It seemed a long way off.

"Martin and I want all of you to come to our place for a big barbecue and pool party," Jane continued after the yelling had died down. "It will be on the Saturday after graduation, from five o'clock till ten o'clock. We'll have swimming, volleyball, singing, and just goofing around. We hope everyone can come, so that's why we're telling you so far in advance. We want everyone to have plenty of time to make their plans. You're welcome to bring any special friends as long as you tell us in advance so we can have enough food for all you hungry monsters!"

The room buzzed with the sound of excited voices, and Kelly's response was as enthusiastic as the rest. She was kind of surprised at her own excitement. Maybe church wouldn't be so bad after all. The youth group certainly did a lot of fun things, and she had to admit all this talk about Jesus was pretty interesting. Not that she had any intention of becoming a *Christian*—she refused to have anything to do with the stuff Peggy had hauled her father into. But she wasn't going to let that keep her from having fun with Greg and the rest of the group. As Kelly began to drift dreamily into thoughts of Greg, she realized Martin was giving the closing prayer. As the class broke up, she caught Greg's eye and he headed purposefully in her direction.

"Kelly, it's good to see you here again."

"Yeah, but it was so embarrassing getting here late. I hate it when everyone looks at you."

"I know what you mean. I've had to do it plenty myself. With three little sisters, one of them is always doing something to make us late. I'm just glad you decided to come."

Kelly flushed with pleasure that he was glad to see her. Greg had managed to find her every day this week at school, even if just for a few minutes. Twice he had walked her to class, a few times he had caught her before the bus took her home, and once they had shared a table in the lunchroom. Most of the time their talk had centered around Camp Sonshine. His parents had given him permission to apply also. They had confided in each other how much they wanted the jobs.

One thing Kelly hadn't mentioned was that one of the biggest reasons—if not the biggest—for her wanting the job was to be near Greg. Their relationship had definitely not progressed far enough for her to be *that* honest. She knew he liked her, but she had the uncomfortable feeling that her resistance to Christianity was putting a barrier between them. The day they had spent lunch together, he had actually bowed his head and prayed before his meal. She couldn't believe he had done it right in the middle of the lunchroom where everyone could see! True, no one had paid much attention, but Kelly was embarrassed. Then, he had actually watched to see if she would do the same thing. Not her! She had given him a defiant look and dug into her lasagna. He hadn't said a word, but she noticed a shade of disappointment on his face. After a few minutes of silence, she had ventured a question about Camp Sonshine. In the midst of their talking, the awkwardness had disappeared. She liked Greg more than any boy she had ever known, but she wasn't going to play a game for anyone. If he couldn't accept her as she was, then too bad.

"I'm glad I came, too," Kelly said. "That barbecue and pool party sure sounds like fun, doesn't it?"

"I've heard that the end-of-the-year party is always terrific," Greg agreed. "I'm looking forward to it. By the way, have you filled out your camp application yet? They're due by the end of the week, you know."

"I've been super busy this week working my odd jobs and teaching riding classes. I just haven't had the time," Kelly admitted. "I'm passing up going to the barn this afternoon, though, so I can do it. Have you done yours yet?"

"I finished it up last night. It was tough. I had to put a lot of thought into it. Some of those questions about my faith really made me think. I know what I believe, but it was kinda hard to put on paper. Anyway, it's done, and I'm going to put it in the mail in the morning."

Kelly listened in dismay to his words. If the questions about his faith were tough for him, what in the world was she going to do with them? She didn't even claim to be a Christian!

"Listen, I'll see you later," Greg interrupted her thoughts. "My parents are waiting for me to go into church." He started to walk away, then stopped and turned. "How about lunch tomorrow?" His face was eager as he faced her. "I can meet you after third-period French and walk over with you."

Kelly returned his smile and responded warmly, "That sounds like fun. I'll be ready for some friendly

company after hatchet-face Grimsley gets done
with me. She keeps telling me that I'll never learn
how to roll my R's, and I'm afraid she might be
right."

Greg laughed in appreciation. "I know what you
mean. I have her last period, and she gives me all
kinds of grief because I can't get the hang of mas-
culine and feminine nouns. It all seems kinda silly to
me. Anyway, see you tomorrow."

As Kelly turned toward the church, she noticed
that her father and Peggy were watching with amused
interest. As she approached them, Emily sang out in
her high, clear voice, "Kelly, is that your new boyfriend?"

Feeling as if she wanted the ground to swallow
her, she peered over her shoulder to see if Greg had
overheard. Hoping he would be deep in conversation with his parents, she was dismayed to see him
give her an understanding grin as he turned to his
folks.

"I told you once, Miss Nosey, that he is just a
friend. Now pipe down. The whole world doesn't
need to know my business."

"Okay, but he sure is cute and nice, too. His sister,
Stacy, is in my class at school, and she's always talking about her big brother."

Heading into church, Kelly had to admit Em was
right. He definitely was cute, and he was awfully
nice, too. She just didn't want her little sister's big
mouth to ruin her chances with him. Her hopes
were high that she would get to know him a lot
better.

• • •

Coming out of church, Kelly's spirits were soaring. She had the exciting prospect of a summer at Camp Sonshine, she was going to a cookout with the youth group, and best of all, she was meeting Greg for lunch tomorrow at school. Her excitement infected everyone, and the car rang with laughter as they headed for Emily's favorite restaurant.

"Okay, I think I got it all straight," her father told the guy behind the counter. "We'll have four jumbo cheeseburgers along with two orders of fries and two orders of onion rings. Add to that four large sodas. We'll come back later for our ice cream."

Kelly slid into the booth beside Emily, and Peggy sat across from them. Her father waited for the tray of food he had just ordered.

"I'm real excited about your possibility of working up at Camp Sonshine." Peggy smiled brightly at Kelly. "I love that place. You know, that's where I became a Christian. In fact, I was your same age."

Kelly bit back the sharp retort that sprang to her lips. Everyone was in a good mood, and Kelly didn't want to spoil it by saying what she really felt about Peggy's Christianity.

"I hope I get the job. It would really mean a lot to me." Her father saved her from having to say anymore by arriving with the mountain of food.

"Hey, Kelly, now that no one can hear, are you gonna tell me all about Greg? He's soooo cute!"

Kelly smiled tolerantly at her little sister. "Honestly, Emily, he's just a friend." Hesitating, she admitted with a grin, "Not that I wouldn't like him to be more. He *is* awfully nice. He's applying for a wrangler position at Camp Sonshine, too. I'll just have to wait and see."

Her father reached across the table and took her face in his hands. "Yes, I guess my little girl is growing up. And getting prettier every day. Are you sure that this Greg fellow is good enough for you? You're pretty special, you know."

"Oh, Dad!" She knew her father was teasing her about Greg, but she was pleased by his compliments. She longed for the days when it was always like this with her father. Back then, he would have already known everything about Greg. For his sake, Kelly tried to keep the atmosphere light.

"Greg invited me out to see his horse sometime and go riding. Do you think you could take me sometime soon? I'd really love to see his horse."

"Not to mention Greg himself, huh?" Her father tousled her hair playfully and then grinned. "Sure, honey, I'll take you out there. This week is going to be real busy with some house closings, but I think we can squeeze it in next week. By the way, when do you need to have the application for Camp Sonshine in? Don't we have to sign it?"

"Yeah. I'm going to work on it today. I want to have it in the mail by tomorrow. I told Mandy I couldn't make it to the barn because I want to make sure I have plenty of time to do it right."

Peggy smiled at her and offered, "You know, I have a lot of experience filling out camp applications. I worked at several camps through high school and college. If you need any help, I'll be happy to share my expertise with you."

Her smile was so warm and her offer so sincere that Kelly found herself responding with the same warmth. "Thanks, Peggy, I would..." She suddenly stopped short. She couldn't accept help from her! She had made a vow not to accept Peggy, and she was determined not to break it. "Uh, thanks, but no thanks. I think I can handle it on my own."

Kelly knew her voice was stiff and hard. She couldn't miss the look of hurt on Peggy's face. Peggy managed to give her a warm smile in spite of it. "Okay, Kelly. If you decide you need help after all, just let me know."

Her father threw her a disappointed glance, and the happy atmosphere that had been present all morning disappeared. The rest of the meal was spent in a strained silence, broken only by Emily's recital of what had happened to her in Sunday school.

Forcing down the rest of her hamburger, Kelly felt bad about spoiling the mood for everyone. But why did Peggy have to try and be her friend? Why couldn't she just leave her alone? Didn't she know that Kelly didn't want to have anything to do with her? And why was Peggy so nice to her when all she did was close her out? Did it have to do with her being a Christian?

• • •

Settling onto her bed, Kelly eagerly picked up the application for Camp Sonshine and read through it. For a long period of time the only sound that filled the room was the scratching of her pencil. The questions about her horse experience were easy. She wanted to make sure she answered them right, though, so the people doing the hiring would be impressed. She knew her application wouldn't look so good when she got to the questions about her faith, so she had to do her best on the first part. Finally they were as complete as she could make them. She reluctantly turned to the second part.

How long have you been a Christian?

Only the first question and she was already stuck. She certainly couldn't tell them that she wasn't one and had no intention of becoming one. That would definitely not land her the job. But what to say? She had gone to church when she was a kid, and she remembered her dad saying she had been christened. Setting her lips firmly, she wrote, "Have been a Christian since I was a small child." *Not impressive*, Kelly thought, *but it will have to do.*

Describe your relationship with Jesus Christ.

The questions were getting harder, not easier. She wasn't sure how to describe something that didn't exist. Searching through her mind, she settled on what Martin had said this morning. She was glad she had listened for once. "Jesus Christ is my best friend. He gave his life so that we could be friends."

Why do you think you would be a good addition to Camp Sonshine?

What kind of a question is that? Kelly wondered. She wasn't sure how she could answer it without sounding like an egotistical pig. Finally she wrote, "I love horses and kids, and I'm a good worker. I get along well with people, and I am very responsible. I have already had a lot of experience doing what I will be doing this summer if I'm hired."

Kelly stretched her tired muscles and released a big yawn. Looking at the clock she was amazed to discover she had been working on the application all afternoon. The shadows in her room were long, and she could hear preparations for dinner downstairs. Gradually the sounds from the kitchen drifted up to her.

"Daddy, come see what Peggy did! She made me a butterfly out of the rest of the cookie dough!"

Emily's excited voice followed by her father's warm laugh brought a smile to Kelly's face. She could picture the happy family scene downstairs. It had been that way when her mother was alive, and Kelly had been an eager part of it. Even after her mother had died, she and her father and Emily had shared some great times. But no more.

Kelly fought the longing she felt to join in the family fun. She stubbornly stiffened her resolve and renewed her vow not to accept her new stepmother. It didn't matter that Peggy could be really nice. She was an intruder.

As Kelly listened to the happy chatter, it became more important than ever that she get the job at Camp Sonshine. She just had to get away for the summer.

EIGHT

I 've been wanting to talk to you." Mandy joined Kelly in the stall she was raking out. "Grand-daddy just got a load of new horses in. There's a big palomino that I think you will really like. He's green-broke, but I think he has great potential to be an awesome jumper, and he's *big!* I know you'll be buying your own horse this fall, if you get that job. I thought you might want to start working with this horse before you leave and maybe buy him when you get back. What do you think?"

Mopping the sweat from her forehead, Kelly leaned against her pitchfork. She had been working hard on the townspeople's stalls, and she was grate-ful for the break. "That sounds great. I'll be happy to work with him, but I've still got my heart set on a big, *black* horse who's fast as the wind. Such a horse may not exist, but I'm going to look hard before I give up."

Mandy laughed and settled herself against the wall of the stall. "I understand. When I was just a kid, I dreamed of owning a flashy white pony with a silver mane and tail. We lived in a small town though, and the best my dad could do was a small brown pony with two white socks. I loved him with all my heart, but sometimes I still dream of my white pony. Tell you what, I'll keep an eye out for your big and fast and *black* horse and let you know if I find such a creature."

Kelly turned back to her work. Mandy watched in silence for a few minutes. "Are you about done here?" she finally said. "I'm eager to try out some of those new horses, and I know you want experience in training. I thought you and I could take out some of those new guys and see what they know. Granddaddy took all of them from the trader because he got such a good deal, but he's going to resell the ones that I say will take too much work to become class horses. It'll probably take us a while, so I'll treat you to dinner and then give you a ride home."

"I would love to help you." Kelly's voice was full of enthusiasm. "You know I want to learn how to train. I want to learn everything I can!" Glancing around, she continued, "I've got one more stall to do after this and then I'm done. It should take me about twenty minutes. King here is a real slob, but Jasmine, next door, is a neat little thing and always deposits her business in one corner. It shouldn't take me long. I'll find you when I'm done. And thanks for the dinner invite. I'll call home and let them know."

Digging into her job with renewed energy, she polished off King's stall and moved into Jasmine's. Her mind was working rapidly. All the hard work she was doing was making her bank account grow steadily. At this rate, with the money she might make this summer at camp, she would be able to buy not only a horse, but also the tack. She already knew exactly what she wanted. She spent a lot of hours dreaming at Hansen's Saddlery.

Blinded by the bright sunshine after so much time in the dim barn, Kelly almost ran into Mandy as she was leaving.

"Easy there, girl. I was just coming to let you know that I called your home. I talked to Peggy. That's your new stepmother isn't it?"

"Yeah. Why? Did she say I couldn't stay?"

"Hey, don't get all riled. She said it was fine and that she hoped we had fun. Sounded like a pretty nice lady. What's wrong? Don't you two get along?"

Not wanting to ruin the day with talk of Peggy, Kelly just shrugged it off. "She's okay." Taking Mandy's arm, she headed purposefully for the barn. "Come on. I want to try that golden giant you were telling me about."

Mandy looked at her quizzically but decided to drop the subject. She allowed herself to be led into the barn.

• • •

"The trader said all these guys had been ridden," Mandy told Kelly, "but we're not taking any chances. The first few times we ride, we'll stay in the arena. That way they can't take off. With a green-broke horse, it's best to expect the worse, so that you're prepared for trouble."

"Do you think some of these horses might be mean?"

"No, not *mean*," Mandy reassured her. "They just haven't learned what people expect of them yet, so it's hard to predict how they will react. The more you work with them, the more they understand what you want, and the easier it is to depend on their actions. I just don't want to give them a *chance* to get us into trouble." Taking her reins in her hands, she smiled easily. "Let's see what these guys know." Placing her left foot in the stirrup she leapt lightly into the saddle. Her mount, an average-size bay, moved restlessly but quieted quickly under her touch.

Following her example, Kelly prepared to mount Nugget, the big palomino Mandy had told her about. He was so tall that Kelly had to strain to reach the stirrup, but once she had it, she sailed into the saddle as easily as Mandy.

"Good work." Mandy smiled at Kelly's success. "He's by far the biggest horse we've ever had out here. He must be closing in on seventeen hands. If he turns out as good as I hope, I may use him for the high jump competition this fall. As big as he is, those jumps should be a piece of cake to him."

Kelly sat easily in the saddle. For the moment, Nugget was standing quietly. He was a beautiful horse and she was impressed by his size, but pictures of her own black creature filled her mind. Leaning over, she gave Nugget a quick pat on his muscular neck and whispered in his ear, "We're learning together, boy, so go kinda easy on me, please."

"Just follow my example, Kelly. By the time we're through, I'll have a pretty good idea whether these fellows are going to work out."

Mandy moved off at a steady walk. Squeezing gently with her legs, Kelly moved Nugget in behind her. She was careful to keep enough distance between them so that in the event Mandy's horse should kick, she and Nugget would be clear. The next hour was spent in executing half and full circles to determine their reining ability—both at a walk and trot—and lots of stopping and starting to judge how responsive they were. Any horse with a hard mouth would not be accepted as a class horse at Porter's Riding Stables. Granddaddy was proud of his string of horses. He had the reputation of having the best riding horses around.

Mandy reined her mount to a standstill. "Let me see you take Nugget through the pattern we've been doing. He's done fine following Rocket here, but I want to see him in action by himself."

Kelly knew that Mandy would not only be judging the horse but her as well. She was determined to make a good showing. Taking a firm grip with her legs, she moved Nugget into a trot. He trotted off easily. She had to admit that his gaits were surprisingly smooth for a horse of his size. Kelly took him through the turns and circles with grace. His body was a little tight from nervousness, but as they continued their pattern, he relaxed more and more. Nugget moved eagerly and kept one ear cocked back to let her know he was paying attention. His circles weren't perfect and there were moments when he broke from a trot into a ground-eating walk, but he was willing. Kelly knew Mandy would be pleased. Finishing the last circle at a full trot, she brought him to a halt in front of where Mandy sat, mounted on Rocket.

"Very nice, Kelly. You kept him going, but you didn't push him too hard. He's a willing and eager horse. He just needs to be given time to learn what we expect of him. Pushing him too hard would only make him resent us. He's got some learning to do, but he's definitely one that we'll keep. In fact, I think I may make him my personal horse since you're going to hold out for your black dream horse. I have some plans for this guy!"

Swinging down from the saddle, she pulled the gate open and led Rocket through. Kelly followed close behind. She was hungry, but there was still a lot of work to do. The two horses had to be groomed, watered, and fed before they could be put out for the night. Only then could she think of herself.

"Aren't you supposed to be hearing from that camp soon?" Mandy asked as they walked. "How long has it been since you sent in the application?"

"Two weeks. I'm looking for an answer any day now. Of course, it won't be anything final. They're going to narrow it down based on the applications and then notify us about a personal interview."

"Well, if they have any sense, they'll hire you. I'm just sorry that you might not be around for the summer. I've started to count on you more and more. You're getting to be a fine horsewoman."

Kelly was pleased and embarrassed by Mandy's words but didn't know how to respond. Smiling gratefully, she turned to Nugget and began to energetically rub his body with the rubber currycomb. Snorting his pleasure, he lifted his head and curled his upper lip in ecstasy. Finishing his rubdown, she led him into his stall where dinner awaited and then filled in the time while he ate by cleaning his tack. She knew Granddaddy would be pleased, and she liked to do it when she had the time.

• • •

"Thanks again for dinner and the ride home. I had a lot of fun!"

"You're welcome. And thanks again for the help. You did a great job." Mandy shifted the stable truck into first gear and eased down the quiet street.

Turning toward the house, Kelly sniffed the night air appreciatively. The darkness was heavy with the sweet perfume of honeysuckle. They had a whole hedge of it bordering their driveway. Her dad had wanted to cut it out because it spread out of control so quickly, but Kelly had fought to keep it. On nights like this she knew the aroma would fill her second-story bedroom. She loved to lay there and drink it in. Humming to herself, she picked up a ball that Emily had left in the yard, and then slipped into the house.

"Dad! Peggy! She's here! Can I give her the letter?" Emily bounded down the stairs and ran up to Kelly. "You got a letter from that camp today. I wanted to open it, but Dad and Peggy wouldn't let me. I've been dying to know what it says!"

Her father was laughing as he entered the room. "Of course we wouldn't let you open it, young lady. That letter is for Kelly, and she's the only one who will open it. I'm glad you're home, though," he admitted with a grin. "There have been moments when I wanted to open it myself."

Kelly looked around eagerly. "Where is it? I thought it would never get here!" Once the letter was in her hands, however, she hesitated.

"What's wrong, Kelly?" Emily asked.

"She's been waiting for this letter, Emily," Peggy joined the conversation, "and she's just hoping it isn't bad news."

Kelly looked at Peggy, surprised that she understood how she felt. Peggy encouraged her with a warm smile, and Kelly tore into the letter. Silence reigned in the room as she absorbed the contents. She came to the end and realized everyone was waiting expectantly for her reaction. They didn't wait long.

"Yes! It's a letter from the head wrangler, and she says that out of forty applicants I have been chosen to be one of the fourteen invited up for a final interview in two weeks! After the interview, they will hire six of us. Can you believe it? I might just get this job after all!"

Spinning around the room, Kelly collapsed into her father's arms. He gave her a big hug. "I knew you could do it, honey. Once they see you in action for themselves, they'll hire you for sure!"

"You bet they will, Kelly," Peggy added. "Congratulations on getting the interview."

Kelly grinned. "Thanks, Peggy."

Her father smiled happily at the fact that she had included Peggy in her joy. Kelly knew that he really wanted them to be friends. She was too excited to show any resentment toward Peggy tonight, so she smiled happily back.

The phone rang, interrupting their impromptu celebration. Emily raced off to get it.

"Kelly! It's for you! It's your new boyfriend, Greg!"

Peggy intervened quickly. "Emily, hush! You don't need to announce your opinions to the world. It would have been quite enough to tell Kelly that Greg is on the phone." Laughing, she shook her head helplessly. "You'll understand in a few years. In the meantime, how about serving the cherry pie I fixed for dessert? Now that Kelly's here, we can dig in."

Casting Peggy a quick glance, Kelly reached for the phone. *She sure does understand a lot,* she thought.

"I got the letter asking me up for the final interview! How about you?" Greg's excited voice pushed all thoughts of Peggy out of Kelly's mind.

"Me, too! Can you believe it? We got chosen out of forty people! I can hardly wait to go up there."

"What do you mean, can I believe it? Didn't I tell you a few weeks ago that they couldn't pass up such multitalented people?" He tried to sound very smug and self-assured, but his excitement won out. He almost shouted into the phone, "Man, I can hardly wait to go up there either. The way Martin talks about it, it sounds like something really special. I thought I would be miserable this summer, being away from all my friends and the rodeos in Texas, but I'm pretty excited." His voice dropped, and he spoke quietly into the phone. "I'm really glad you got selected for the final interview, too. I hope we get to work together for the summer."

"Me, too." Kelly stammered a little as she spoke into the phone. *He was hoping they would work together! Oh man, she just* had *to get that job.* She brought her thoughts back to the phone as Greg continued.

"One of the reasons I called is about the interview. How are you getting up there?"

"I guess my dad will take me up." Looking questioningly at her father, she was relieved when he grinned and nodded. "How come?"

"Well, both of my folks will be out of town that weekend. They have some business convention to go to. If I was in Texas, I'd have plenty of relatives to call who could help me out, but I'm kinda stuck. Do you think I could hitch a ride with you and your folks?"

"Hold on a sec." Covering the mouthpiece, Kelly addressed her father. "Dad, Greg's parents are going to be gone the weekend of the interview and he needs a ride. Can we take him with us?"

Her father smiled and pretended to consider Kelly's request. "Well..." He threw his hands up in the air to protect himself from the fierce glare she sent his way and laughed. "Sure, honey. It takes about three hours to get there from here, so we'll have to leave about seven in the morning to get there in time. We'll pick him up on the way out."

"Thanks, Dad." Kelly turned back to the phone. "Dad says he'll be happy to do it."

"Great! Well, I have to go learn some more French nouns. I don't want to give Grimsley a chance to jump on me tomorrow! You want to have lunch again? We have a lot of plans to make. I could pick you up outside of your French class."

"I'd love to! Thanks for calling. See you tomorrow." Humming to herself, Kelly quietly slipped the phone back into its cradle. It had been a great day. She had been asked by Mandy to help train the new horses, she had been selected for the final interview, and Greg was hoping they would work together for the summer. And in just two weeks the three of them—her dad, herself, and Greg—would head for Camp Sonshine. It had been a long time since she had spent time with her dad, and she was looking forward to it.

"Kelly, come in the kitchen! I've got the cherry pie and ice cream all ready for us to eat."

Kelly smiled at the sound of her little sister's eager voice. She was sure her father was making Emily wait until she joined them. Cherry pie was just the right thing to celebrate with. Skipping into the kitchen, she settled into her chair and enthusiastically dug into the steaming pie.

Her father watched her for a moment and then said cheerfully, "We'll make arrangements for Emily to stay over at her friend's house so all of us can head up to Camp Sonshine for your interview. Peggy says it's been years since she's been up there."

Kelly slowly put her fork down and stared at her father. Some of the warm glow she had been feeling all evening slipped away. "But Dad! I thought just you and me would head up there. Does Peggy have to . . ." Her voice faded away as Peggy stepped back into the kitchen with the fresh napkins she had gone to get.

Her father's voice was firm and unyielding, and his look was one of clear disappointment. "We're all going up, Kelly."

Kelly knew there was no use in arguing, especially with Peggy in the room. Getting away from home for the summer was looking better and better. *Maybe by some huge stroke of luck,* she thought angrily, *Peggy will disappear by the time I get back.*

Peggy stopped and looked from one to the other in concern. "Is there a problem?" She couldn't hide the hurt in her voice, and Kelly felt a twinge of guilt at her meanness.

Rising from the table, Kelly's father slipped an arm around Peggy's waist and said in a reassuring voice, "Of course not! We were just talking about how much fun it would be going up to Camp Sonshine. Didn't you tell me you hadn't been there for ten years?"

Looking from him and back to Kelly uncertainly, she responded with a feeble smile, "Yes, it's been a long time. I'm looking forward to seeing the place again."

Suddenly losing her appetite for the cherry pie, Kelly shoved her chair back from the table. "It's been a long day and I'm pretty tired. I think I'll go on up to bed. See y'all in the morning." Silence followed her as she headed up the stairs. Reaching her room she collapsed gratefully on her bed.

• • •

Refreshed by a shower, Kelly leaned against the windowsill and drank in the perfumed air. The night was bright with the glow of a full moon. The only sounds that broke the stillness were those of crickets and bullfrogs singing from the creek bank. She went over in her mind the letter she had received that day, trying to imagine what the interview would be like. She had no idea what to expect, but had gotten this far and would just have to do her best. Even if she didn't get the job, at least she would have a whole day with Greg! Her father and Peggy would be there, but she imagined Peggy would keep her dad from messing things up.

Stopping short, Kelly realized that her last thoughts

of Peggy had been positive. Peggy *had* shown tonight that she knew what it was like to be a teenage girl, Kelly considered. And she had been great about Emily yelling out that Greg was her boyfriend. But why did she have to be her stepmother? Out of habit, Kelly renewed her vow not to accept her.

Turning her thoughts back to the interview, she felt confident in the fact that she would do well on anything regarding horsemanship. She wondered if they would ask more stuff about Jesus and Christianity. She determined to listen closer in church and Sunday school for the next two weeks. She might need some of the language they used. She had obviously fooled them on the application, so she was fairly confident she could get through the interview.

Realizing that her eyes were heavy, Kelly crawled into bed. Her last thoughts were of Greg and meeting him for lunch tomorrow. Her dreams that night revolved around Greg and herself working together at Camp Sonshine.

NINE

Good morning, honey. Did you sleep well last night?"

"Dad! How can you possibly call this a good morning? It's raining outside. Why *today*, of all days?" Kelly rubbed sleep from her eyes as she entered the kitchen. "And no, I hardly slept at all last night! I'm *so* nervous. What if I mess up the interview and don't get the job?"

Her father, with laughter in his eyes, answered in a calm voice. "Don't act like it's the end of the world. You won't mess up the interview. You're a fine horsewoman. You'll go up there and do your best. We'll be proud of you, no matter what happens. As for the rain, this is normal for April. I can almost guarantee that the sun will be out by the time we make it to camp." Moving away from the stove where he had been stationed, he said in a teasing tone, "Now come eat your breakfast. We have to be on the road in thirty minutes. Greg will be waiting for us."

"Breakfast! How can you possibly think of food at a time like this? I'm too nervous to eat a thing. Maybe just a glass of orange juice."

Peggy appeared in the kitchen in time to hear her last remarks and laughed. "I know how it is to be nervous, but you really need to eat. Your father has fixed a great breakfast. You certainly won't be able to do your best if you're hungry all morning. It's a long time till lunch, you know."

Kelly grudgingly admitted that she was right. Her father would have just demanded that she eat. Peggy had actually made it seem like a smart idea. Pulling up her chair, she dug into steaming scrambled eggs, savory sausage, and the spicy applesauce Peggy had made that week. Kelly's stomach was still turning flips from nervousness, but she felt better able to handle them.

As she ate, Kelly reviewed everything in her mind. The blue jeans she had on were worn, but still looked nice. She had considered wearing her jodhpurs, but hadn't wanted anyone to think she was putting on airs. She wore a crisp, white shirt under her pale blue sweatshirt. Sneakers completed her outfit. She had her riding boots stowed in the trunk of the car and had even thrown in an additional work shirt. Not knowing what to expect from the interview, she was prepared for anything.

• • •

Shaking raindrops from his hair, Greg collapsed into the backseat beside Kelly. "Whew! It's really coming down out there. I sure hope it stops before we get to camp. How much riding can we do in *this* stuff?"

Greg had dashed out to the car as soon as Kelly's dad had pulled into the driveway. His eyes were still sleepy, but to Kelly he looked wonderful. He wore blue jeans, too, and his red sweatshirt contrasted nicely with her blue one. They had talked the night before about what to wear. They weren't sure what would be best, so they had decided to go the same. At least they would be possible oddballs together.

Kelly's father laughed and offered the same encouragement he had given Kelly. "This is pretty typical of April. I can almost guarantee you that the rain will be stopped by the time we get to camp. In the meantime, help yourself to the doughnuts that Peggy picked up last night."

Greg blinked in surprise. "Hey, how did you know I'd be starving?" He grinned appreciatively as he stuffed the doughnut in his mouth.

"I didn't. Peggy insisted we get them last night because she thought with your parents out of town that you wouldn't fix anything for yourself. She hated the idea of your going through the whole morning hungry."

Greg's voice was full of admiration. "Gosh, Mrs. Marshall, you sure got that right. Mom and Dad left food, but I was too sleepy and nervous to mess with it. Thanks a lot for thinking about me."

Kelly was astonished. That really had been sweet of Peggy to think of Greg. That was the way her own mom had been, she realized. At the thought of her mother, her eyes began to burn and her throat got a catch in it. She missed her mother even more now that Peggy was around to remind her of things her mother used to do. No one could take her mother's place, though, and she certainly didn't intend on letting Peggy think she could.

Greg turned to her, and Kelly smiled as she forced a natural tone. "Are you as nervous as I am?"

"I'm sure I'm supposed to say I'm not, but it's only honest to admit that I have a lot of butterflies in my stomach." Greg grinned sheepishly. "It took me forever to get to sleep last night because I kept imagining what it would be like."

"Me, too. Of course, I don't really think you have much to worry about. With all your experience, you'll get the job for sure. They'd be crazy not to hire you."

"They'd be just as crazy not to hire you! You've been teaching for so long, and you have all that jumping experience. I bet we both get the job."

Kelly and Greg grinned at each other in the confines of the backseat. Kelly's dad's voice broke in on them. "Well, if a mutual admiration society has anything to do with your chances, neither one of you has anything to worry about." Laughing, Peggy agreed.

The time passed swiftly as they tried to imagine everything possible that could happen to them during the interview. As they drove, the foothills gradually grew into tall mountains. The last hour was spent on tiny, winding roads that offered glorious views of the surrounding peaks. Thirty minutes from camp the sun broke through, just as Kelly's dad had predicted. The air was crystal-clear and the leaves glistened with the remnants of the morning rain. Wild dogwoods dotting the hills were in full bloom, and the riotous colors of spring wildflowers were everywhere. Rounding one particularly tricky curve, they were rewarded with the roaring splendor of a waterfall. Cascading down onto jagged rocks, it caught the rays of the early-morning sun and changed them into glorious colors. Kelly and Greg were silent as they took in all the beauty. Their hunger for the jobs at Camp Sonshine grew.

"Five more minutes and we'll be there." Peggy's excited voice broke into the silence. "I'd recognize that old oak tree anywhere. I used to look for it every time I came to camp. I knew when I saw it I was just minutes away from days of fun!"

Kelly and Greg looked at each other with delight and apprehension. The big day was here at last, and so much depended on it.

The last five minutes were spent in a downward spiral on the mountainous road. As they rounded the final curve, Kelly gasped at the beauty spread before her. Their descent of the mountain had emptied them into a tree-dotted valley graced by a large lake. One side of the road was dominated by a lush green pasture that was home to several dozen horses. Their gleaming coats spoke of good health. The herd consisted of several bays, shining chestnuts, a couple of golden palominos, and even some colorful Appaloosas. A quick glance told Kelly that there were no black horses. Obviously she wouldn't find her dream horse here.

As Kelly's dad slowed the car, Peggy spoke with the excitement of a little girl. "There's the sign for camp. It's a little weathered, but the camp refuses to replace it because it was painted by a young counselor who died of leukemia. I didn't realize how much I had missed this place." Shifting in her seat, she glanced at Kelly. "The horses look great! There's more now than there were when I came here. You'll find that this camp takes excellent care of its animals."

Kelly responded enthusiastically. "It sure looks like it. I'm glad, too. I couldn't work for a place that didn't treat their animals well." Her voice filled with awe. "I didn't realize this place would be so beautiful! The mountains, the lake, the pasture, everything..."

Her words trailed off, and Greg spoke up eagerly, "Martin told me this place was something else. He didn't exaggerate! Spending the summer up here would be like heaven."

Rounding a curve, they spotted a large parking lot full of young people dressed like themselves. Kelly and Greg exchanged looks of relief. At least they wouldn't look like oddballs.

As Kelly's dad parked the car, he whispered loudly, "Good luck, you two. If you ask me, y'all are a shoo-in. Try and have a good time!"

Kelly and Greg responded with a nervous laugh. Kelly leaned over and gave her dad a quick kiss as she climbed from the car. "Thanks for bringing us, Dad. You can count on us doing our best. You and Peggy have a good time, too."

"Hello!" A pretty woman with long, curly blonde hair and a contagious smile walked up to them. "You two must be Kelly and Greg. Welcome to Camp Sonshine. My name is Susan. I'm the head wrangler. You're the last to get here, so we'll head to the barn and then take care of introductions."

As the quiet group headed after her, they exchanged curious glances. The few people who knew each other stuck together. Kelly was glad she had Greg. It made her feel less conspicuous.

Emerging from the wooded trail, Kelly got a good look at the barn. Its red paint gleamed brightly in the morning sun. It was obvious it had received a new coat for the upcoming summer. There were several hitching posts lining the front, and the large paddocks behind it were well shaded. Several hundred feet away a tall, tin-covered building towered over them. Kelly guessed it was the hay barn. Martin had told her they produced their own hay for the animals. Entering the dimness of the barn, Kelly noticed that everything was neat and orderly. She was impressed and also knew she could count on a lot of hard work if she was hired for the summer.

Kelly swung her attention to Susan, who had begun to speak. "Let's go around and introduce ourselves. Then I'll tell you more about Camp Sonshine and what the wrangler's job is like. I imagine all of you are a little curious about that."

Everyone laughed nervously. As they went around the circle telling their names, Kelly examined them. Which ones would be hired for the summer? Were there people here who were better with horses than she was? Would they have better answers about Jesus than she did? They all looked nice, and she found herself wishing that all of them could get the wrangler jobs. She was realistic though. She knew they wouldn't all be hired, so she was going to try her hardest to make sure *she* was!

After everyone introduced themselves, Susan began to tell them about the camp. "Camp Sonshine has been here for twenty-five years. I imagine some of your parents came here first as campers and later as counselors." She smiled as several kids nodded their heads.

Kelly kept still. After all, Peggy was *not* her parent as far as she was concerned.

Susan continued, "This camp is a very special place. We take the responsibility of our campers very seriously. We want them all to have a good time, but first we have to keep them safe and in one piece so that they can. Working with the horses, our wranglers have to keep safety foremost in their minds. All of you are here because I was impressed with your experience, but you can't afford to let the simple fact of safety leave you even for a minute."

Susan paused to let her words sink in and then continued, "Camp Sonshine was established to give children an opportunity to know Jesus Christ. Everything we do is aimed toward that goal. The kids come because of the horses and the other fun things. We use their being here as an opportunity to share Jesus with them. You may have opportunities to share with them personally, but your real job is to be a horse wrangler and that will take up most of your energy."

That suited Kelly just fine. A horse wrangler was all she was. She had no intention and certainly no desire to share Jesus with anyone. Maybe she would be able to avoid all the Jesus stuff...

"Even though you won't be talking much with the kids about Jesus, you will do a lot of talking with me," Susan said, much to Kelly's dismay. "Every day we will have Bible studies and pray together. I want your summer here to be a time of growth for each of you who are hired as wranglers." She smiled, then spoke in a brisk, businesslike voice, "Now, let me tell you about your jobs. If you get hired as a wrangler I guarantee that you'll work hard. Each of you will teach four classes a day, each class lasting an hour. You will teach the level of class that I think you'll be most comfortable with. An additional hour will be spent doing necessary barn work. I won't tolerate a messy barn, and I have high standards. You'll be in teams of three that rotate for morning feedings. On your team days you'll have to be in the barn by six o'clock. The day doesn't end until five-thirty in the afternoon when the horses have been fed and let out for the night. Any questions?"

She softened as she looked at all the intent faces surrounding her. "It won't all be work though. We'll have plenty of time for fun. You'll have two hours of free time every day to do what you want, and most of the evenings will be yours. There is an Olympic-size swimming pool, canoeing and skiing in the lake, archery and riflery, and the best crafts department in the state. At night there will be special functions for the staff—parties, dances, cookouts, midnight swims, etc. I think everyone will have a good time. We work hard but we also play hard."

Kelly and Greg exchanged looks of delight, and everyone else seemed to relax a little. No one was afraid of hard work, and certainly everyone loved to have a good time.

"The first thing we'll do is some work in the arena," Susan announced with a grin. "I need to find out what your teaching skills are like, so I'm going to let each of you teach. You'll have ten minutes to teach a mini-lesson in whatever I assign you. First, though, we have to get the horses ready. I want you to get a real feel for a day around here, so the horses are still outside, waiting to be fed. We'll feed and groom, and then tack them up. That way I'll really see you in action."

The next hour the barn was a beehive of activity. The horses were let in to eat, and the stalls were cleaned. Then all the horses were groomed. While they worked, everyone took the opportunity to get to know their fellow applicants. Kelly discovered that several people were from out-of-state. All of them seemed to have impressive horse experience. The only thing that might give her an edge over her competitors was that she had more experience than anyone else in the jumping field. She hoped it would make the difference for her.

When all the work was done, Susan called them back together. Kelly noticed that Greg made a special effort to work his way over to where she was standing. With a warm glow, Kelly listened to Susan's words. "Good work, team. I can already tell that I'm going to have a hard time deciding which ones to hire. We'll head to the arena in a few minutes. I'm going to assign horses. As soon as you get your mounts ready, take them to the arena and begin to loosen up. We'll start the teaching as soon as everyone is there."

Susan began assigning horses, and one by one the hopeful horse wranglers went to work. "Kelly," Susan said when she finally got to her, "you will be riding Ralph. He's one of our few jumpers, and even though he has a dumb name, he's a fine animal. His one drawback is that he can be pretty stubborn. I thought I'd warn you in advance."

Kelly remembered Ralph from the feeding. He was a tall, big-boned bay, who had the powerful hindquarters of a jumper. Hauling Ralph's tack to his stall, she ran the brush over his body once more to give him an extra shine and then tossed the saddle up on his high back, being careful to adjust it so as not to cause any saddle sores. He stood quietly while she worked. Things became more difficult when it came to bridling him. Holding the bridle in the proper position, she held it up to his head only to have him raise his nose straight up in the air. He was so tall that it was impossible to reach him. As soon as she lowered the bridle, he obligingly lowered his head. Lifting the bridle for another attempt, Kelly was dismayed when his nose went straight back up.

Playing this game for several minutes, she was aware that one by one the others were leading their mounts to the arena. Horrified that she would be last, Kelly desperately searched her mind for a solution. They could play the game they were playing all day, and Ralph would be a certain winner. Her only chance was to outwit him. She looked around for something to stand on, but could find nothing. Noticing a can of grain that had accidentally been left behind, an idea sprang to her mind. Looping the bridle over her shoulder, Kelly reached for the grain and poured it in Ralph's feeder. As he greedily lowered his head and began eating, she slipped up beside him and, before he realized what was happening, had the bit in his mouth and the bridle securely over his ears.

"Bravo, Kelly!" Susan cheered from where she had been quietly watching. "I see you have Ralph all figured out. I think you've been the fastest ever to figure out how to get a bridle on his stubborn head.

I hated to do that to you, but watching you convinces me you know horses. Good job!"

Kelly flushed with pleasure at Susan's words. Looking around she noticed they were the only two left in the barn. Maybe Ralph had done her a favor by being so stubborn!

Exiting the barn, Kelly noticed Greg waiting for her. He was sympathetic as she joined him. "Tough luck!" he whispered. He brightened, though, when Kelly told him what Susan had said. His sympathetic look changed into a grin. "See, I knew you'd show them how good you are."

Falling in step beside Greg as they led their horses to the arena, Kelly marveled at her good fortune. She had a chance for this job, and Greg was showing more and more interest in her. It would almost seem too good to be true if they got to spend the summer together.

The rest of the morning passed swiftly. Kelly had been assigned the job of teaching the posting trot, and she knew she'd done a good job. She taught it for four hours every Saturday. She was lucky that she had gotten such an easy topic. Some of the other riders had not been so familiar with their topics and had seemed to flounder during parts of the lesson. Greg had done as well as she. He had been assigned to teach everyone the beginning elements of running the barrels. His response had been a pleased grin, and he had charmed everyone with his easy, confident manner.

Their next activity had been to take a long trail ride all the way around the property. The camp was large, and it took them an hour and a half. During that time, Susan had the chance to view them at a walk, trot, canter, and even a small stretch of galloping. Ralph's gaits were smooth, and he was very responsive to Kelly's slightest touch. He may be stubborn, but she was forced to agree with Susan's assessment that he was a fine horse.

• • •

"I don't think I've been this hungry in my whole life!"

Kelly was too busy piling the food on her plate to reply to Greg's outburst. She agreed wholeheartedly, though. It seemed like a lifetime since she had eaten her dad's cooking that morning. She was determined to do justice to the lunch that Dennis, the camp cook, had prepared for them. Mounds of fried chicken and piles of thickly sliced, smoked country ham were spread on the long wooden table in the rustic old dining hall. Huge bowls contained ample servings of potato salad, baked beans, and fruit salad. Loaves of hot, homemade bread were sending off an irresistible aroma. Pans of frosted brownies were at the end of the table, and Kelly could hear the motor of an electric ice cream maker coming from the back. If all the food at camp was going to be this good, she would have to watch her weight, even with all the hard work.

Weaving through the tables, Kelly and Greg made their way to the long table where the other job applicants were. Judging from the looks of their plates, they were starving, too. So much had happened. After the lessons and the trail ride, everyone had come back to the barn. The horses had all been unsaddled, cooled off, and groomed before being put back out to pasture. Evidently they were to do no more riding, but Susan had not yet given them the schedule for the afternoon. Silence reigned at the long table as the hungry wranglers proceeded to demolish the feast.

"Okay, everyone. By the looks of the amount of food y'all just put away, you are going to need a break before we get back to work!" Susan grinned teasingly as several of Kelly's group nodded and groaned. "You'll soon learn that Dennis is the best camp cook this side of the Mississippi. Don't be surprised if you can't fit into your jeans by the end of the summer. I promise you won't be the first!" Pausing, she looked around the group approvingly. "Y'all did some fine work this morning. Take the next half hour and wander around camp. That will give you a short rest, and you'll also get a closer look at Camp Sonshine. Make sure you're back at the barn by two-thirty. Have fun!"

The rest of Camp Sonshine was as beautiful as Kelly dreamed it would be. Careful landscaping had been done, and the grounds were an oasis of greenery and flowering plants. The cabins were made of rustic logs and contained enough bunk beds to house eight campers and two counselors. Each cabin was nestled back into the woods where the trees formed a protective arbor for them. The rest of the buildings were also constructed of the same rustic logs. Care had been taken to make sure they blended into their surroundings. The Olympic-size swimming pool sparkled in the sunlight, and Kelly looked at it longingly.

Greg caught her wistful look and grinned. "I know it looks wonderful, but it's still pretty early in the spring for mountain swimming. There haven't been enough hot days to warm the water yet. I have a feeling that water would be something of a shock."

"Yeah, I guess you're right. Still, it will be nice this summer. If..."

"If we get the jobs, you mean. After today I want this job more than ever. I can only hope it's God's will for me to spend my summer up here. If not, I guess He has something better. I can't imagine what, though! I feel pretty good about how the morning went. How about you?"

"It's so hard to know, but I'm pretty sure I did as good as everyone else. I wonder what Susan has for us this afternoon. It's close to two-thirty. We better head to the barn."

Strolling over to the barn, Kelly thought about what Greg had said. He had hoped it would be God's will for him to spend the summer there. Did God really control things like that? She didn't know. She could only hope that she and God wanted the same things.

Back at the barn, Susan outlined the events of the afternoon. "The next three hours will be spent in a couple of ways. One, I want to use this time to get to know each of you better, so I'll be calling you each into my office for about twenty minutes to chat with you. The rest of the time you'll be doing the chores that I hate to do." With laughter in her voice, she looked at the group. "I always love it when applicants come. I get more work done than at any other time of the year. All the stalls need to be cleaned and filled with fresh sawdust, the saddles and bridles need to be cleaned, and several of the horses need minor medical care." Gazing around, her eyes settled on Kelly. "Kelly, can you and Greg take care of the first aid before you dig into the other work? It's nothing major—just some cuts and scratches that need to be treated. There's a list in the tack room of the injured animals, and I'll show you where we keep the medicine."

"Sure, we'll be glad to do it." Kelly felt good when she noticed Susan's pleased look.

Kelly looked up from Sugar's leg when she heard Susan call her name. The time had flown, and Sugar was the last horse to receive treatment.

"You go ahead, Kelly," Greg said. "She's ready to talk to you now. I'll be praying that all goes well."

"Thanks. You'll be next, then. We're the only two who haven't talked to her yet." Stretching her arms over her head, Kelly yawned. "It sure has been a long day. Bed is going to feel good tonight. See you in a few minutes." Smiling cheerfully, Kelly headed for Susan's office. She had put up a good front for Greg, but inside she was nervous. What if she didn't answer Susan's questions good enough? What if she blew it during these next few minutes? All day she had been striving to remember all that she had learned the last couple of months in church and Sunday school. This job was just too important to blow it now.

"Come on in, Kelly." Susan looked up from her desk and waved her to a chair. "Sit down while I finish this last set of notes. I'll be right with you."

Kelly used the few minutes to gaze around Susan's office. The walls were covered with prints of the horses of the world—graceful Arabians, stocky quarter horses, elegant American Saddlebreds, flashy Thoroughbreds, powerful draft horses, and the colorful Appaloosa. On Susan's desk was a large plaque that read, "I can do all things through Christ who strengthens me." Susan cleared her throat, and Kelly gave her full attention.

"Thanks for doctoring the horses for me. I wasn't sure I would have time to do it today, and I don't want to neglect any of them. From the way you handled the horses today, I was pretty confident you could manage it."

Kelly smiled and flushed at Susan's sincere compliment.

Susan smiled warmly and continued, "I'd like to use the next few minutes to get to know you a little better. It's not enough time, but I have to do the best I can in the amount of time I have. You answered this question on your application, but I'd like to know a bit more. Tell me about your relationship with Jesus Christ."

Here it was—the *big* question. Kelly swallowed hard. Forcing a confident note in her voice, she answered carefully, "Well, my family has never been much on going to church, but just a few months ago we started going regularly. I'm part of the Sunday school there, and now Jesus is my best friend!" Pausing, Kelly thought desperately. Surely there was something else she could say. She finally blurted out, "Oh yes, and I was christened as a child." She halted in confusion, and then not knowing what else to say, just waited. She was aware of Susan's shrewd look, but she couldn't read her expression. Susan's next question was a surprise.

"Tell me something about your family, Kelly."

Feeling more comfortable, Kelly relaxed. "My dad is great. He has his own real estate company in Kingsport where I'm from, and almost everyone knows him. My little sister, Emily, is a good friend. She's four years younger than me, but we're really close. I'm lucky to have such a neat family."

When she stopped, Susan looked at her quizzically. "What about your mother? Wasn't there a woman in the car with your dad when he came this morning?"

"Oh yeah—that's Peggy. She's not really my mother, just my stepmother. She and my dad have been married about three months now. She used to come to camp here as a kid and wanted to see the place again, so she came with us."

"How do you get along with Peggy?"

Susan's quiet question, coupled with the sincere caring in her voice, almost caused Kelly to spew out her resentment. She caught herself just in time. She couldn't tell Susan what she *really* thought. Her answer was deliberately evasive. "Oh, we get along okay. I stay pretty busy, so I don't really see her very much."

Susan fixed her with a steady gaze but didn't push her any further. "Okay, last question. After being here for a day, why do you think I should hire you?"

That question *again*, Kelly realized. She looked down, giving herself a few seconds to get her thoughts together. She was fairly sure that she hadn't impressed Susan too much with her first two answers, so she had to do her best on this one. Lifting her eyes back up to the head wrangler, she forced a confident note into her voice, "I've only been here a day, but I already love the place. I like the way you take care of your horses and barn. I'm a hard worker, I love horses and children, and I've had a lot of experience teaching and leading rides. If you hired me for this job, I can promise you that you wouldn't have a harder worker." Breathless, she waited for Susan's response. She had done her best.

"Thanks for your honesty and all your hard work, Kelly."

Kelly couldn't help but cringe at her words. If Susan could know how far from honest she had been, she'd probably kick her out of her office.

"I'll tell you what I told all the other applicants," Susan continued. "You'll be hearing from me within two weeks, regardless of my decision. It will take me a while to make my choices. Thanks for coming up, and I'll be in touch with you soon." Susan smiled warmly. "After I talk to Greg, everyone will be free to leave. Have a good trip home."

TEN

Kelly's mind felt numb as she pushed open the heavy door to the school entrance and emerged into the bright sunshine. Her last-period class had been algebra, and the midterm exam had been a tough one. She had studied hard and felt like she had done well, but her mind was exhausted. Today was her day at the barn, and she was looking forward to the exercise and fresh air. It was just what she needed after a hard test.

"Hey, Kelly! Have you heard anything from that camp yet?"

Looking up, Kelly saw her friend Julie. "Not yet. I've raced home from school every day this week hoping for an answer, but it hasn't come. I didn't really expect anything last week, but Susan said we would have an answer within two weeks. Today's Wednesday, so I only have three more days to wait. Maybe there will be something today. Anyway, I'll let you know as soon as I know something."

Heading toward the bus that would drop her by the stables, Kelly was startled by the honk of a horn and someone calling her name. Looking around quickly, she was astonished to see the family wagon with Peggy at the wheel. Frightened, she dashed toward the car.

"Is something wrong with Dad? Is it Emily?" Her voice was breathless from the fear she felt. Something had to be wrong. She could think of no other reason for Peggy to be there.

Peggy laughed as the wide-eyed girl slid into the car. "Take it easy. Nothing is wrong. I'm sorry if I frightened you, but I thought you would be rather eager to read this." Smiling, she handed Kelly a letter that bore the distinctive Camp Sonshine logo.

Slowly Kelly reached for it. Holding it in her hand, she could do nothing but stare at it. What if it was bad news? What if she hadn't gotten the job? She didn't want to cry in front of Peggy. She would want to go off and be alone.

Peggy seemed to read her mind and spoke reassuringly. "Go ahead and open it, Kelly. I'm sure it's good news. I have a good feeling about it."

Kelly sat a little straighter. Taking a deep breath, she tore open the envelope. A quick glance set her thoughts whirling. "I got it, Peggy! I got the job! They really want me. I can hardly believe it!" Grinning from ear to ear, she turned excitedly to her stepmother and before she stopped to think about her actions, reached out and gave Peggy an exuberant hug.

Peggy responded with a quick hug of her own and then broke in on Kelly's ecstatic thoughts. "One more little thing you might be interested in..." Pausing deliberately, she smiled mischievously. At Kelly's questioning look, she grinned and said, "I called

Greg's mother just before I left. He had to leave school early for a dentist appointment, so he has his letter already. Greg got the job, too!"

Kelly collapsed against the seat. It was too good to be true. She and Greg, working together at Camp Sonshine! She pinched herself to make sure she wasn't dreaming and yelped at the pain. Certain she was awake and that all this was really happening, she dimly realized that Peggy was talking again.

"I knew you had been wanting to see Greg's horse, Shandy, so Greg's mother and I thought I would take you over to Greg's stable for the afternoon. Your dad and Greg's father will meet us there after work. They're going to bring a big bucket of fried chicken to celebrate. How does that sound?"

Suddenly, Kelly remembered who was talking. This was *Peggy*. Why was she being so nice? A voice inside Kelly reminded her that accepting Peggy's offer would only weaken her vow to reject her stepmother. Yet today Kelly was just too happy. She had the job at Camp Sonshine with Greg, and she was going to celebrate by spending the whole afternoon with him. She could take advantage of Peggy's kindness—it didn't mean she had to accept her.

"That sounds great," Kelly replied. "Thanks for arranging all of it. I was headed out to the barn anyway, so I have everything I need. Let's go!"

Determined to forget, for the afternoon at least, her feelings about Peggy, Kelly chattered all the way out to the Lazy B Stables. She planned, out loud, all the things she would need to do before she could head for camp at the end of school. "I'll have to talk to Granddaddy Porter so he can find someone else to handle all the beginner classes. And I'll have to talk to Mandy so she'll know I can't keep training the big palomino. Oh, I'll have to talk to all the town boarders, too, and let them know I won't be able to clean their stalls this summer." Pausing, Kelly thought of Greg. A whole summer with Greg! Clothes! She would need some new clothes for the summer. Turning to Peggy, she asked, "Do you think Dad will let me buy some clothes for the summer? It's been a long time since I've spent much money on clothes."

Laughing, Peggy reassured her. "I know your father will be pleased to buy you some clothes. He's just been waiting until you wanted to wear something besides worn-out blue jeans. You'll be wearing a lot of those at camp, but you'll also need some nice clothes to impress Greg."

Kelly marveled once more that Peggy could understand so much. As they approached the Lazy B, where Greg kept his horse, she stopped talking and looked around curiously. She had only been out to the Lazy B once, and it had been several years before.

As she gazed around, Kelly was thankful for Granddaddy's strict requirements for Porter's Stables. While Porter's was neat and organized, the Lazy B looked like no one cared. The grass was unkempt, and several boards in the surrounding fences were rotted away. Pieces of tack and grooming equipment were lying all around, and the barnyard had an uncared-for look. How could Greg stand to keep his horse at a place like this? Did they care for the horses well enough?

As though he knew she was thinking about him, Greg suddenly materialized. Emerging from the darkness of the barn, he dashed over to the car. "Howdy, fellow camp wrangler!"

Pushing aside her dislike for the Lazy B, Kelly responded with enthusiasm, "Howdy yourself, fellow camp wrangler!" As she got out of the car she was enveloped in a big bear hug. Blinking in astonishment, Kelly could only stare at Greg. Forcing herself to speak lightly, she grinned up at him and said, "Can you believe it? We both got the jobs!"

"You of little faith! How many times did I tell you that they would be crazy not to hire such talented people? When they saw us in action for themselves, they just couldn't resist us."

"Ha! I noticed that you rushed home from school every day the last two weeks to check your mailbox, too. If you were so sure of yourself, why were you so anxious?"

"Well, you can never be too sure of people, you know. They might not have been able to recognize natural talent right under their noses." His cocky words were tempered by an excited grin. "Come on! I want to show you Shandy. He's spent the afternoon getting handsome so he would be ready to meet you."

A little dazed, Kelly turned to follow him.

Peggy gave a slight cough and reminded Kelly of her presence. Red with embarrassment, Kelly caught Greg by the arm. "Wait a minute. Where is your mom? She and Peggy are supposed to get together here."

Flushing equally red, Greg leaned over the car window. "Gosh, Mrs. Marshall, I'm really sorry. I'm not usually this rude. I'm so excited about us getting the jobs, I lost all my manners. Mom is over there in the clubhouse." Grinning ruefully, he said, "It's not much, but at least it's air-conditioned."

Peggy smiled in understanding, "Don't worry about forgetting me. I understand perfectly. I envy you two the opportunity to spend a whole summer at Camp Sonshine. Have a good time riding. We'll have the food all ready when y'all get back."

Turning away, Kelly and Greg moved toward the barn. "You wait out here. Shandy wants to show off in the sunshine."

In just a few moments, Greg emerged proudly from the barn, leading one of the most beautiful horses that Kelly had ever seen. Shandy was a powerfully built gelding. He stood almost sixteen hands high. His well-formed head tossed pridefully in the air, and his buckskin coat glistened in the afternoon sun. He was a beautiful animal, and he knew it. He danced lightly in place for a few moments, then grew quiet and stood still as a statue so that she could catch all of his splendor.

Clasping her hands together, Kelly spoke fervently, "Oh, he's wonderful. You told me he was beautiful, but I didn't expect this!" Extending her hand she moved slowly up to his proud head. "Hello, Shandy. You're really something, aren't you?" He gazed at her disdainfully for a moment, then snorted his agreement. Only then did he lower his head to accept her strokes. He stood quietly for a few moments, and then butted her playfully with his head as if to cement their friendship.

"See, I knew he'd like you! He doesn't like many girls, but I knew he'd like *you*." Greg grinned at her and continued proudly, "Shandy is one terrific horse. We used to win most of the calf roping contests in our area back home in Texas. He's a whiz at running the barrels, too."

"And you trained him yourself? That's my dream. To have a horse all my very own that I can train from the beginning. With the money from this summer, I'll have enough to buy my horse when I come back in the fall. I can hardly wait. Especially after seeing Shandy. You've done such a good job with him."

Greg grinned and spoke with modesty. "He was pretty easy to train. He's one smart horse—aren't you, buddy?" As he spoke he rubbed Shandy lovingly on the neck. "Anyway, I've got a great little mare saddled for you in the barn. Let me go get her, and we'll go for a ride." Looking around he admitted, "I know the barn isn't much, but there is a lot of land around to ride on, and that pretty much makes up for it. I was pretty spoiled in Texas with all the open space, but at least I get to have Shandy with me. My folks thought at first that I would have to leave him behind. I had to work hard the last few months we were there to make the money to get him up here. But we're together, and that's all that matters."

Kelly stared at him with undisguised admiration. This was truly a boy after her own heart. She could sense her feelings for him growing stronger and stronger. She could only hope he felt the same way. His hug in the parking lot had given her hope, but only time would tell.

• • •

"Hey, let's race! See that big oak tree in the far right corner of the field? This is the biggest open area on the place, and Shandy loves to let it all out. Are you game?"

Kelly looked dubiously at her little mare. Christy was a sweet little horse and very responsive, but she didn't stand much of a chance against Shandy. Still, it was all for fun. "You're on! The loser has to do the other's French homework!" Laughing, she urged Christy to a full gallop before Greg had even moved. Kelly knew she would lose, but she would at least get a head start.

Hearing Greg's startled shout behind her, Kelly leaned close to Christy's neck and urged her on. The little mare was fast, and she was enjoying the run. Concentrating on the exhilaration of the wind flying in her face, Kelly was only dimly aware of the sound of pounding hooves growing closer.

"You got your head start, but you don't stand a chance against Shandy!" Greg tossed the words out laughingly as Shandy moved up beside Christy. He hunched down closer to his horse's neck as Shandy opened the gap between the two horses.

Kelly kept a steady hand on Christy's reins but was able to study Shandy and Greg as they flew by. It was obvious they were a team who had been together a long time. She felt an intense longing for her own horse rise up in her. As she galloped along she dreamed that she was on Crystal. They would fly through this pasture like the wind, neck and neck with Greg and Shandy. She could just imagine the fun that the four of them would have.

"You're really a good rider," Greg said as she rode up. "You got more speed out of little Christy than anybody ever has. I have to tell you that Shandy is the fastest horse on the place. No one has ever beaten us."

Pulling Christy down to a halt under the spreading arms of the huge oak, Kelly laughed up at Greg. "Don't worry. I didn't think we would win. But you just wait! When I get my own horse, there won't be anyone that can beat *us!*"

Shandy was still fired up after his run and was obviously eager for more. Greg talked to him soothingly until he settled down. Then, together, Kelly and Greg turned their horses toward the barn at an easy walk. Glancing around, Kelly was struck by the beauty of the afternoon. The sun was slowly being swallowed by the towering trees, and the air was aglow with a soft orange light. The surrounding oaks and pines cast enormous shadows that seemed to envelop them as they moved in and out of the waning sunlight. The air was sweet with the perfume of honeysuckle and wild roses. Looking over at Greg, she marveled they were sharing this together. He looked so strong and handsome as he proudly rode his beautiful horse. Kelly could hardly believe all this was happening to her. She could only hope that nothing would mess it up.

"I sure am glad you came out this afternoon. It was great of your mom to suggest we all get together. She seems like a pretty neat lady."

Abruptly, Kelly brought her thoughts back to what Greg was saying. She was irritated that he wanted to talk about Peggy. "Yes, it was nice of Peggy, but she's not my mother. She's just my stepmother."

"Sure, I know. But why make such a big deal about it? She's still a neat lady." He was silent for a moment. "I've noticed sometimes that you two don't get along too well," he said at last. "How come?"

Looking down, Kelly struggled to control her emotions. Her hopes for the perfect afternoon were destroyed. Why did Greg have to bring up the subject now? They were alone, and he wanted to talk about Peggy! Swallowing her disappointment, she tried to answer him honestly. "My mom and I were real close. When she died it was hard, but Dad, Emily, and I pulled together and we made it. In fact, we did just fine and became really close. When Peggy came along, everything changed. Dad and I aren't close like we were, and everything revolves around *her*."

Greg glanced at her and chose his words with care. "I think I understand what you mean. But I've watched Peggy, and she seems to really want to be your friend. Wouldn't it make it easier for you if you would let her be?"

Kelly had heard enough about Peggy. She knew Greg didn't understand. Shrugging her shoulders, she answered in a tight voice, "You have no idea what it's like. It's not quite as easy as you like to think it is." Couldn't he just shut up about Peggy? Couldn't he just enjoy being with her? Why all the questions?

Greg was still regarding her quizzically. "You know, Kelly, the bitterness in you will only hurt you."

Glancing at him sharply, Kelly kept quiet.

Continuing, Greg said, "Jesus can take that bitterness away from you."

Kelly had just about had it. First Peggy, now Jesus. She groped around for something to say that would get Greg off the subject, yet not upset him or make him think bad about her. Forcing a smile, she responded lightly, "Hey, cool the Jesus talk. I'm just not ready, okay? I appreciate what you're saying, but all I can do is ask you to pray for me."

Greg tried unsuccessfully to hide the disappointment in his voice. "I'll be happy to pray for you because I really care." Pausing for a moment, he said in a troubled voice, "I hope you know what you're getting into this summer. There is bound to be a lot of Jesus talk at Camp Sonshine. I think you're going to have a lot of big decisions to make before the summer is out. I'll always be here if you want to talk."

"I'll remember that," Kelly said quietly. Wanting to end the conversation, she added, "In the meantime, I think there is some chicken back at the barn with our names on it. I don't know about you, but I'm starving!"

Trotting slowly back to the barn, nothing more was said about Peggy or Jesus. They talked lightly about what they had to do before they left for the summer. The magic of the afternoon had been lost—because of Peggy.

ELEVEN

Kelly, where have you been?" Emily shouted down the stairs as Kelly wearily pushed the kitchen door open. "The phone has been ringing for you all morning, and Greg has called every thirty minutes since noon. I'm tired of answering the phone all the time."

"Sorry, Emily," Kelly apologized. "My last beginner class ran over some this morning because the little girl's mother brought me some cookies as a going-away present. Then Sara, the girl who's teaching for me this summer, had some last-minute questions. Not to mention saying goodbye to Granddaddy, Mandy, and all the horses. Anyway, I'm home now. I'll get the phone when it rings next time." Tossing her riding boots on the stairs leading up to her bedroom, Kelly turned to the refrigerator. "What's for lunch? I'm starving."

"Dad, Peggy, and I ate about an hour ago, but Peggy left you some spaghetti on the stove. It should still be hot. She and Dad ran out to get you some last-minute things you need before you leave tomorrow."

Tomorrow! She, Kelly Marshall, was actually just hours away from leaving for Camp Sonshine. The weeks since the acceptance letter had flown by. They had been crammed with chores, teaching, riding, buying all she needed, and spending time with Greg. Nothing else had been said about Peggy between her and Greg since that day at the stables. Greg still met her after French class every day and walked her to lunch, but Kelly was sure she sensed a difference in his attitude toward her. She was certain that her refusal to talk about Peggy and Jesus had something to do with it. Maybe this summer she would find out how Greg really felt about her. He was always sweet to her, but she couldn't help noticing that he seemed to be waiting for something before he let them get too close.

Sitting down at the table, Kelly had just swallowed the first mouthful of spaghetti when the phone rang.

"See!" Emily yelled as she came running down the stairs. "I told you it's been ringing all morning. Bet you the last piece of cherry pie that it's Greg!" Emily materialized around the corner and glanced wishfully at the refrigerator.

"No way! I've been dreaming about that pie all morning. Now scram—I want to talk to Greg in private." Wiping off her mouth, Kelly eagerly picked up the phone. Hearing Greg's voice, she was glad she hadn't let Emily con her into that bet. Peggy's cherry pie was delicious, and there would be no more for ten weeks.

"I thought you would never get home! I've been calling for the last couple of hours."

"I know. It took me longer at the barn than I thought, but at least I got everything taken care of. I even got to feed Smokey his special carrot. I had promised him something special before I left. What's up, anyway? Is something wrong?"

"No, nothing's wrong," Greg responded a little sheepishly. "I can just hardly believe that we actually leave for Camp Sonshine in the morning. I was calling to talk to you so I would be convinced it's really true."

"Well, it's true. Dad and Peggy are out buying the last few things I need. I just have to add them to the other stuff I've already packed. Dad says it looks like I'm going away for a year. I guess I do have a lot, but I just want to make sure I'm prepared for anything."

"Yeah, I know what you mean. My mom said if I took any more stuff, she and Dad would have to rent a truck to get me up there! By the way, we're still planning to come by and pick you up at five for the pool party at Martin and Janie's tonight. It's a great way to spend the last night, huh? We'll have lots of fun and be able to tell everyone goodbye, too."

Kelly took the last chew of the spaghetti she had crammed into her mouth while he was talking and quickly swallowed. "You're right—it should be great fun. I just looked at the clock, though, and realized how much I have to do before you pick me up. I gotta get moving. See ya in a few hours."

• • •

"Wow! You look really great in that blue sweater. It's new, isn't it?"

Kelly blushed at Greg's compliment. The afternoon had been extremely hectic, and she had just jumped out of the shower fifteen minutes before he had arrived at the door.

"Thanks. Yes, it's new. Peggy helped me pick it out last week."

The last comment had been for the benefit of her father who was watching from his recliner in the den. She knew he would be pleased she had given Peggy the credit for the sweater. Her dad had been great about coming up with the money for the new clothes, but he had insisted that Peggy accompany her to pick them out. Kelly's resentment at Peggy's intrusion had been tempered by the knowledge that she really knew clothes and managed to find what would look best on her stepdaughter.

"You two have fun!" Kelly's dad called from the den. "Remember to be home by ten. You don't want to head up to Camp Sonshine and start your first day tired."

"I'll be home by ten, but I can't promise I won't be too excited to sleep!" Kelly tossed the words over her shoulder teasingly as she followed Greg out the front door.

Kelly was well aware of the admiring glances that Greg threw her way as she conversed with his parents from the backseat of their shiny black Honda. Peggy must have been right when she said that the blue sweater complemented her bright blue eyes and brought her coppery hair to life. Secretly, Kelly was glad for *anything* that would focus Greg's attention on her. Though they were going to be together for ten weeks, there would also be dozens of other girls their age up there, and they would probably be *Christians*. Kelly knew how important being a Christian was to Greg. Even though she had lied to Susan to get the job, she was determined to be honest with Greg.

The hours of the cookout flew by. Martin and Janie had gone to a lot of trouble to make it special. The leafy oaks beside the pool were strung with streamers and balloons. Colorful banners proclaimed goodbye messages to the departing seniors. To Greg and Kelly's surprise, there was also a large banner that read, "Goodbye, Greg and Kelly! Have a Great Summer at Camp Sonshine! We'll Miss You!" Kelly was amazed these people cared so much when she had known them just a few months.

For two hours the yard rang with the shouts and laughter of fifty people. The pool was large enough to accommodate a diving contest as well as a rousing game of pool volleyball.

Martin broke away from the grill long enough to shout, "Okay, all you water rats. Dinner in fifteen minutes—and I don't serve anyone that drips on my new white apron!"

Kelly was starving and was thankful she had crawled out of the pool a few minutes earlier so she was dry. Her copper curls were beginning to dry into their natural shape. All she had to do was pull on her new sweater and the pair of white pants Peggy had picked up earlier in the day. Kelly had been sure that the sweater would be too warm to wear tonight, but she had been wrong. There was still a nip in the late-spring air, and she snuggled her sweater around her appreciatively.

Kelly jumped as Greg's voice sounded above her shoulder. "How nice of you to save a place in line for me. How did you know I would be starving?" Greg had pulled himself out of the water just as Martin had shouted his order, and his wet hair glistened in the lights. He looked great in his white sweatshirt and jeans. All Kelly could do was smile. She hadn't really saved him a place—she had just snagged a spot near the front of the line because she had gotten ready so quickly. With a thrill, she realized several of the other girls in the group were eyeing her enviously. Greg was easily the best-looking guy in the group. Any number of the girls would have been thrilled if he had sought them out.

Feeling a twinge of daring, Kelly hooked her arm through his and flashed a brilliant smile up at him. "It was the least I could do for my summer partner. It would be too bad if you withered up and blew away right before we leave!"

Greg grinned at her appreciatively and drew her closer in to his body. "You are truly a woman after my own heart. Thanks!"

An hour later, the whole group was groaning. There had been double-decker cheeseburgers, baked beans, chips, and pickles for everyone. To top it all off, they had just polished off four canisters of home-made ice cream and five pans of brownies. The lights around the pool cast flickering shadows over the group. Kelly was sure she would be content to never move again. That was until she thought of Camp Sonshine...

"Earth to Kelly! Earth to Kelly! Hey, come on! Snap out of it!"

Greg's teasing voice brought Kelly back to the present. Blushing from embarrassment, Kelly replied laughingly, "I had just made it about halfway around the lake at Camp Sonshine on my dream horse. It's hard not to think about it when it's so close! Can you believe we leave in the morning?"

"We're leaving all right, but first we have to finish up tonight. Martin just called us all together in the den. We're going to do some singing and stuff. If we don't hurry, we'll have to sit on the floor."

The den in Martin's house was large, but it still had a cramped feeling when it was filled with over fifty bodies. Of course there were benefits. Kelly and Greg had gotten the coveted positions on the sofa, but there were so many people sharing it that they were all crammed together. Kelly was finding it very pleasant to be forced into such close proximity with him.

"Okay, everyone—let's make this place shake tonight," Martin said over the noise of the room. "With this many people in here singing, we should be able to make the walls move!" Everyone laughed and cheered as Frank and Scott, two of the graduating seniors, began to warm up on their guitars. What followed was twenty minutes of loud, wonderful singing.

Even Kelly joined in enthusiastically. They were Christian songs, but they were upbeat and fun, and she enjoyed singing. She figured she didn't have to understand or agree with all the words. After the singing was over, Martin picked his way to the front of the room and turned to face them.

"Tonight I thought we would do something a little different. I'm sure most of y'all are tired of hearing me talk anyway!" Martin laughed easily at the cheers that rippled through the room. "I thought we would let some of the seniors do the talking since it will be their last official night with us. I've asked Bonnie, Sandy, Allen, and Jeff to share some of what Jesus Christ has done in their lives. Jeff, why don't you start?"

Kelly wasn't interested in anything they might have to say about Jesus. She managed to spend the next thirty minutes daydreaming about Greg and Camp Sonshine. Greg was listening intently to what was being said, but every few minutes would turn and flash her his gorgeous smile. Kelly was perfectly willing to sit there on the crammed sofa for as long as they wished. She couldn't help listening, though, when Sandy rose to speak. Kelly had admired Sandy for several years. She was very pretty and the vice president of the senior class. She also had a gorgeous Saddlebred horse at the most prestigious stable in the county.

"Being a part of Kingsport Christian Center and this Sunday school class has been the most important part of my high school years," Sandy began.

Kelly listened in wonder. Surely she must be joking, Kelly thought. Maybe she was just trying to make everyone feel good.

Sandy continued. "Most of y'all remember when my mom died back when I was twelve. I missed her so much that I wanted to die, too. I was mad at everyone—especially God. Everyone had always told me that he was a God of love. Some love! I thought. I didn't want to have anything to do with him, and I became really bitter. I shut everyone out.

My father, my brother, my friends—everyone. The only thing that kept me going was the memory of how much my mother had loved me. I was really lonely, though, and I was crying out inside for someone to break through the wall I had put around me. When I turned fourteen, someone introduced me to alcohol, and I learned that on the weekends, at least, I could leave my troubles behind. Thankfully, that only lasted for a year because I was well on my way to serious trouble."

As much as Kelly wanted to tune out what Sandy was saying, she found herself helpless to stop listening. Was this really Sandy? Kelly had never known all this. Sandy had always seemed so together and so in control of things, yet it sounded like she had come awfully close to totally messing her life up. *Something* had changed her.

Sandy took a moment to look around the room and then continued, "Right after I turned fifteen, a good friend who has already graduated invited me to come to church with her. I didn't like the idea of going to church, but I *did* want a good friend. My loneliness was becoming unbearable. Kingsport Christian Center was different from any other church I had been in. After a few weeks I started to really listen to what was being said. As the weeks passed, I was challenged to give God a try and to allow him to show me how much he loved me. The day arrived when I let him break through the walls around my heart, and I invited him into my life. I've never been the same. Oh, I've had bad days, and it took God a while to heal all the hurts, but I know he loves me and that he'll always be there. I can only hope that all of you will learn the same thing."

As Sandy took a seat, Kelly was aware of a battle raging within her. So much of what Sandy said made sense. It was clear that God had made a real difference in her life. Maybe this *was* what she needed, Kelly considered. God could take away the pain of her mother's death. Becoming a Christian would make her father happy, and it might make a real difference in her relationship with Greg. But weren't those selfish reasons? And what about Peggy?

At the thought of Peggy, Kelly felt the old resentment rising up. Kelly had handled the pain of her mother's death pretty well until Peggy had come along. She had been happy with her father until then, too. What did God have to do with all that? All the stuff about God wanting to be her friend was great, but she had been just fine until Peggy came along.

As the final song of the evening was being sung, Kelly had a nagging sense that she did need God—that she needed him badly. But she just couldn't—or wouldn't—let go of the resentment in her heart toward her new stepmother long enough to reach out.

"Well, it's been a wonderful night. All of you seniors feel free to come back and visit us anytime. As for Greg and Kelly, we'll see you two at the end of the summer. Good night, everyone." Martin's words brought the party to a close.

Everyone started talking and hugging friends goodbye. As Greg pulled Kelly up from the couch, she decided that she didn't have to deal with it now. In the morning she was leaving for a great summer at Camp Sonshine. When the summer was over, she had the prospect of her dream horse. There were too many things demanding her attention.

With the brief sense that she was making a mistake, Kelly pushed the thought of Sandy's words out of her mind and turned her attention to Greg and her friends.

TWELVE

Good grief! I feel like I've been run over by a truck. I'm so sore I can hardly move. Could we have possibly only been here twenty-four hours? I'm not sure I'll live long enough for the kids to arrive in two days!" With a groan, Tina collapsed on the bed.

Feeling sympathy for her bunk mate, Kelly stretched and rolled over so that she could hang her head down from the top bunk and talk. "I'm beat, too, but at least I'm used to this type of work because of my job at Porter's. I'm sure it will get easier as we toughen up." Kelly was aware that even though Tina was an excellent horsewoman, she had never worked regularly in a stable. Tina's parents were rich, and most of the manual work was done by a hired hand. Tina would get used to it. She would have to. Here, *they* were the hired hands.

It was hard for Kelly to believe that she had been at Camp Sonshine only a little more than twenty-four hours. Susan hadn't been kidding when she told them they would be busy. *Busy* was hardly an adequate word!

Staff members had started pouring into camp at eight the previous morning. The caravan consisting of her and Greg's cars had pulled in at nine. Susan had been there to meet them and direct them to the staff quarters where they would be housed for the summer. The girls' staff cabin was separate from the boys', but they were located right next to each other. Kelly's cabin was home for all the girl staff members who weren't regular counselors sleeping with the campers. Twice as large as the regular cabins, although with the same rustic decor, it had room for sixteen girls. This summer it was full. There were three girls, including Kelly, working with the horses, three girls helping in the kitchen, three girls operating the craft room, two girls supervising the waterfront activities, two girls running the country store where the kids went for drinks and candy, two college-age lifeguards supervising the pool area, and finally, Susan heading up the whole situation.

So far everyone seemed likable and friendly, and Kelly was looking forward to becoming better friends with everyone in the cabin. Yesterday there had been time for little more than introductory chit-chat, and last night everyone had collapsed into bed with little more than good nights. One hundred twenty eager campers would be pouring into Camp Sonshine in just two more days. There was not only a lot of work to be done, but a lot of training to take place as well. Kelly found it hard to believe all of it could be done in two more days, but Susan had reminded them that the camp had done it this way for years and everyone always lived through it. As

Kelly stretched her aching muscles, she wasn't too sure.

A sharp knock at the door brought a chorus of groans from the girls in the cabin. They were grabbing a precious thirty minutes of rest before dinner was served. "Hey, Kelly, you're closest to the door, so you get the honors!"

"Some honor," Kelly grumbled at the anonymous voice coming from the dim interior. She wearily swung down from her bunk and opened the door.

"Kelly! I thought you might like to..." Hesitating, Greg took a closer look at Kelly. "You look awful tired. Were you resting? I can come back later when the dinner bell sounds."

The sight of Greg standing in the doorway, freshly scrubbed from a hot shower, caused Kelly to forget all about her tiredness. Smiling at him brightly, she said, "I *was* resting a little bit, but I'm fine. What did you want?"

"We have about thirty minutes before dinner, and I thought you might like to take a short canoe ride on the lake. It's really pretty this time of the day, and I saw a bunch of fish jumping when I went by a minute ago. Would you like to go?"

"That sounds great! I've been dying to get out on that lake. Hold on while I put on my tennis shoes. It will only take me a second." Kelly's enthusiastic response brought a pleased glow to Greg's face as he turned to sit on the balcony railing of the porch.

"Now that's what I call a smooth operator. While the rest of us are up here checking out the quality of available men, Kelly brings her own."

Turning in the direction of the amused voice, Kelly recognized Patty, one of the girls helping in the kitchen. "Greg is just a friend," Kelly told her, but she couldn't help smiling. "We're part of the same youth group back at home, and we go to school together. He's not my boyfriend." *Yet*, she finished silently to herself. Kelly could only hope that the summer would make the difference in their relationship.

"Yeah, well anytime you want to get rid of your *friend*, just let me know. I wouldn't mind going canoeing with him before dinner." Kelly laughed at Patty's envious voice and ran out the door.

Falling in place beside Greg as they headed down to the lake, Kelly thought once more about how lucky she was to be here. Looking down at her, Greg spoke in a friendly voice, "I probably should have let you rest, but next to horses, my favorite thing is the water. I've really been wanting to get out on the lake." He paused for moment and then said in a quiet voice, "And I wanted to take you with me."

His words filled Kelly with a daring she hadn't known before. She took his arm as she smiled up at him. "I'm glad you came and got me. I've been with you all day, but you've always been at the end of a shovel, a wheelbarrow, or a horse. We really haven't had a chance to talk. What do you think of this place so far?"

"I think they know how to get work out of a person! The last twenty-four hours remind me of the summer I spent working for my uncle on his ranch in West Texas. For the first week or so, I didn't think it was possible to live through it. But I did, and by the end of the summer the hard work didn't bother me." Greg was laughing as he steadied Kelly stepping into the canoe.

"I know what you mean. I thought I worked hard at Porter's, but I'm beginning to think I don't know the meaning of the phrase *hard work*. It's okay, though. I'm so happy to be here that hard work isn't going to bother me. Just think, we'll be here for ten whole weeks."

"Yeah, and we'd better make the most of it because it will be over before we know it. You know, I already love this place. Listen to how quiet it is."

"For two more days, anyway." Kelly gave a rueful grin and then fell silent, quietly absorbing the beauty of the afternoon.

The lake was so calm that she could see herself and Greg reflected in the mirrorlike surface. The sun was just slipping below the horizon. Before departing, it had kissed the fluffy clouds with a rosy hue. The toads and crickets were tuning up their orchestra, and in the distance she could see a large bass break the water in search of his evening meal. Kelly detected a movement at the far end of the lake and focused her gaze on the grove of trees protecting the far cove. As she watched, she saw a small band of five horses push their way through the undergrowth and move into the lake. Lowering their heads, they buried their velvety muzzles in the water and enjoyed a long drink. Satisfied, four of them turned back for shore but the fifth, a large bay named Samson, had something else in mind. Raising his head from the water, he lifted it high and snorted water everywhere with his flaring nostrils. Lifting his right front leg high from the water, he began pawing defiantly. Finally satisfied that all was okay, he stopped and stood still. Then, as if in slow motion, he lowered his massive body into the water and enjoyed a good roll. Kelly could see his legs kicking in the air as the water flew about. After a few minutes he stood up, walked from the lake, and then broke back through the underbrush to join his friends.

Filled with delight, Kelly looked to see if Greg had caught the performance. His laughing eyes told her that he had. He spoke quietly so as not to break the spell, "Shandy loves to do that same thing after a hard, hot day. He gets his back scratched and gets cooled off at the same time." Digging his paddle into the water, Greg sent the canoe shooting toward shore. "If I'm not mistaken, the dinner bell should ring in five minutes. I, for one, am ready to eat half of the dining hall. I do *not* want to be at the end of the line."

• • •

"Okay, everyone. Gather around." Susan smiled at the tired faces that encircled her. "Y'all have done a tremendous amount of work in just three days. I'm very proud of you. The campers will be arriving in the morning after breakfast. The first riding classes will start after lunch tomorrow."

As Susan talked, Kelly reflected on all that the group had accomplished in just three days. Everyone's riding and teaching ability had been tested again, and they had been given their teaching assignments. Kelly was confident in her area. She was to be in charge of all the English and jumping classes. During the class periods that no one wanted to ride

English, she would handle the beginner Western classes. Greg was to teach all the games and rodeo events and would also handle some of the intermediate classes.

Susan's voice broke into Kelly's thoughts. "I believe that as a group y'all are the most qualified wranglers that I have had the privilege to work with here. I'm looking forward to having a great summer. Now remember—I'll be up with you for feeding this week, but only until you get comfortable with it. Then you're on your own. While y'all are slaving away, I'll be snoozing away."

She laughed as their good-natured protests filled the air. "Hey, there have to be some benefits to being responsible for such a motley crew! You don't think I do this for the money do you?" Reaching out for Kelly's hand, she spoke through her grin, "Everyone link up and let's give this whole operation to Jesus. He's the one who will make sense out of all the chaos that will fall on us tomorrow."

Kelly bowed her head but her thoughts were on the square dance that was being held for the staff that night. They had actually hired a bluegrass band for the event. Staff members from the previous summers had assured her there would be plenty of good food and fun. She had never danced with Greg before and was looking forward to it. Kelly had already decided what she would wear tonight. Her brand-new jeans would be perfect. Peggy had bought her a bright blue Western shirt that was the exact shade of the sweater she had worn the night of the cookout. She was confident Greg would like it. To set off the tan she had acquired in the past few weeks, she had a white silk bandanna to go around her neck.

Susan's amen broke the group up, and everyone headed toward their respective cabins.

They had twenty minutes before dinner, and then they would have an hour to get ready for the square dance. Greg was caught up in conversation with the other guy wranglers, so Kelly allowed herself to drop behind the group. She wanted to think for a few minutes.

Even though her brain felt crammed with information, Kelly was very peaceful. The problems of Peggy and home seemed far away. It had been hard to say goodbye to her father and Emily, but Kelly was glad to be out of the pressure-cooker situation. All she had to concern herself with now was remembering the feeding and work schedules. She knew there was really nothing to worry about. Time would make them habit. Time would also make her familiar with the maze of trails that crisscrossed the camp and meandered through the mountains. She was looking forward to exploring them all during her free time. That was one good thing. Susan always kept several horses who were still a little green-broke out of classes. The wranglers had the freedom to ride them whenever they weren't teaching classes or doing barn work. Susan had said it not only kept the wranglers happy, but she was also presented with well-trained horses at the end of the summer.

Unbidden, Kelly's thoughts turned to Crystal. She smiled happily at the thought of buying her horse in the fall. She still had to find her, but she was confident that somewhere her dream horse waited for her. Humming lightly to herself, Kelly joined the group just as the dinner bell sounded and smiled happily at Greg as he slipped up to her side.

THIRTEEN

Kelly emptied the contents of her grain can into the last horse feeder and straightened with a sigh. Leaning back against the door of Samson's stall, she gazed out across the empty pasture as he dug into his well-earned dinner. The peace and quiet that reigned over the barn was a welcome respite after the hustle and bustle of the day. Two weeks of classes, trail rides, and early feedings had indeed toughened her. She was tired at the end of the day, but not to the point of exhaustion. There was still enough energy for fun, and Kelly had made plans to join the rest of the wranglers for a swim before dinner. The pool would be empty of campers by now, and the staff was free to use it.

"Hey, Kelly! Quit daydreaming and hurry up. We only have an hour before dinner, and we want to enjoy the pool."

Kelly smiled absently at Tina and said, "Y'all go ahead. I'll be up in a few minutes. I want to experience the barn *quiet* for a few minutes."

"Whatever you say. You can experience all the quiet you want. I prefer to experience the cool water of the pool closing over my body." With a laugh, Tina turned away and joined the rest of the wranglers heading toward the pool.

Sinking down into the sawdust outside of Samson's stall, Kelly leaned her head back against the solid wood and closed her eyes. The only sound that filled the air was the munching of hungry horses after a hard day's work. Their eager crunching covered the distant sounds of clanging pots in the dining halls and the shouts and voices of one hundred and twenty small campers. For now, it was just Kelly and the horses. Kelly settled back and allowed the peace of the barn to envelop her being.

The last two weeks had been as wonderful as Kelly had anticipated. She loved working with the kids and had experienced the thrill of coaching several youngsters over their first jumps. She remembered the exhilaration of *her* first jump. It was fun to watch the kids develop their confidence as she taught them. The trail rides were small—just a cabin at a time—so they were a piece of cake. At least when all the horses behaved.

On Kelly's first official trail ride, the group had stopped at the edge of the lake to give the horses their customary watering. Water-loving Samson had decided he was hot and needed a dip. Heedless of the young boy's cries, Samson had pawed the lake and then nonchalantly laid down to roll in the refreshing water. Kelly had yelled instructions to the little boy, and he had been able to step clear to safety. Urging her horse forward, Kelly had grabbed Samson's reins as soon as he stood up. Leading him out of the water, she had helped the boy mount back up.

The rest of the group had been in hysterics. Not wanting to hurt the little boy's feelings, Kelly had remained serious. At least until he started laughing. Then she had joined in and everyone had roared. Kelly had been sure to compliment the little boy on how he handled it, and he had become the star of the cabin. Susan had just laughed when she heard the story. Once every few weeks, Samson would get in the mood for a swim and nothing could stop him. So far, thanks to capable handling by experienced wranglers, the only negative results had been muddy saddles.

Samson, as if knowing he was being thought about, chose that moment to stick his head over the stall door and blow in Kelly's hair. He was finished with his dinner, and now he wanted some company. Absently reaching up to stroke his velvety nose, Kelly fell back into her dreamlike state.

Camp life outside of the barn was wonderful, too. The girls in the staff cabin had knit together as a group, and Kelly had developed several close friends. She and Tina were especially close and spent hours talking about any and everything. Tina was especially curious about Greg. So was Kelly! She knew that Greg made a special point to be with her— joining her at meals, playing with her in the pool, sitting beside her at staff Bible studies—but he remained so darn *friendly!* He had never once tried to take her hand, put his arm around her, or anything. Kelly knew he liked her a lot. She still had the feeling he was waiting on something before he let them get closer.

In the meantime everyone was having a wonderful time. Susan had been right. They would work hard, but they would play hard as well. There was a continuous chain of water volleyball games, ice cream parties, moonlight horseback rides, late-night swims, and plenty of free time to do whatever they wanted. Kelly had begun work in the craft shop on a leather belt for her dad. She knew he would be pleased.

"I didn't know you were still here." Susan's voice startled Kelly out of her dreaming. "Wasn't everyone going up for a swim? I thought I was the only one who lived in the barn."

Looking up, Kelly smiled sheepishly. "Everyone did go swimming. I decided to stay behind for a little while and just enjoy the barn and the horses. It's not often that there aren't a hundred things going on in here. It's so peaceful right now."

Sinking down into the sawdust beside her, Susan responded, "I enjoy it this time of the day, too. I love the activity of the summer, but sometimes I get homesick for the solitude of the off-season. I seem to be able to think clearer when there isn't so much going on."

Kelly nodded. "I know what you mean."

Susan continued, "Since you're here, maybe you could help me with a new horse that's coming in a few minutes. I got a call this morning from the executive director of the camp. He told me that a wealthy landowner in Texas wanted a tax write-off, so he was sending me a horse."

"All the way from Texas?"

"Well, it seems this guy has a daughter who came to camp here years ago and has always wanted her father to do something for the camp. I guess this is it. Anyway, I have no idea what this horse is like, so I could use some help getting it settled. If we miss dinner, I'll get Dennis to fix us something special."

"I'd love to help you out!"

Both of them heard the rumbling sound of the trailer at the same time and jumped up from where they were sitting. Samson threw his head back in protest of being disturbed and snorted his displeasure. Kelly stopped just long enough to stroke his head in apology, and then rushed after Susan who was almost to the door of the barn.

Kelly joined her just as the dusty blue truck came to a halt. While it was dusty, the truck was obviously very expensive—and so was the matching trailer. Emblazoned across the sides of both the truck and the trailer was the name *Southland Ranch*. As the weary-looking driver of the truck climbed from the front seat, whatever was in the back began to kick the sides of the trailer in protest.

"Dadburned horse!" the man growled. "If her highness is not moving forward, she gets all bent out of shape and tries to knock the sides of the trailer out. Guess she figures that wherever we're going, she'll get there faster without the help of this metal contraption. The way she moves, she's probably right." Pausing in his speech, the burly driver reached out and shook Susan's hand. "I reckon you're the missus that runs this operation. The boss told me it was a lady." Looking at the barn and then turning to gaze at the teaching rings, he said in a skeptical tone, "I hope you got a place tight enough to hold this little spitfire."

As if wanting to live up to this description, the horse in the large blue trailer kicked harder.

Trying to hide the concern in her voice, Susan spoke lightly, "I thought we would put her in the stall at the end of the barn. That's where all the new arrivals go."

"Begging your pardon, missus, but I don't think you'll want this little spitfire in a closed-in stall just yet. She'll need to run some of the fire out of her. It's a long ride from Texas, and even though I let her out a few times, I couldn't risk letting her walk around much. She's a handful, this one is!" He looked around once more but didn't seem satisfied with what he saw. "Don't you have any kind of big arena with some tall fences? She'll be out of these small arenas in the shake of a cat's tail."

"Excuse me, Mr..."

"The name is Hawkins. J.C. Hawkins. You can just call me J.C. Everyone does."

"Well, J.C., just what kind of horse have you brought me? I hope the owner of Southland Ranch, Mr. Moncrief, realizes that this is a children's camp. This horse doesn't sound much like a child's horse."

Kelly had been listening to the exchange between Susan and J.C. with growing curiosity. Just what kind of horse *was* in the back of the trailer? From the sound of things, this mare had plenty of spirit. She hoped they would get done with their talking soon so she could lay her eyes on this animal.

"Well, ma'am, I wouldn't rightly say that this filly is a child's horse," J.C. admitted. "Mr. Moncrief just told me that there was a camp in the North Carolina mountains that was real special to his daughter, and he wanted this horse delivered here. Didn't say nothing about this being a children's camp. He just knew a good piece of horseflesh when he saw it and decided to send it to you. His roundup this month was especially large, so it didn't hurt him none to get rid of one of the two-year-olds."

"Excuse me, but did you say roundup? Where did this horse come from?"

"Gosh, ma'am, I thought you knew all about that. Mr. Moncrief, that's my boss, owns about five thousand acres in south Texas."

Kelly whistled to herself in amazement. She couldn't even imagine having a place that big.

"Now as you can imagine, it's a right big job to try and work that much land. What Mr. Moncrief does is turn out one hundred of his top brood mares along with one of his top studs. Once they're out there, he just leaves them be. Then every year, in the spring, he rounds them all up and separates the two-year-olds from the herd. Generally folks are waiting in line for the right to bid on those young'uns at auction. His daughter really laid in to him this year about doing something for the camp, so he picked out this fine little girl and sent her up."

Susan took a deep breath. This time she made no effort to hide the concern in her voice. "Am I to understand that you have brought me a wild, two-year-old filly that has only been off the open range for a few weeks?"

J.C. fidgeted a little under her relentless stare, but answered honestly. "Yes'm, I guess that's the truth of it. Wait till you see her, though. She's really something, this one is. Just needs a little bit of work and attention. Wouldn't mind having her myself."

By this time Kelly was dying to get a look at the horse inside the trailer. Moving away from Susan, she began to edge toward the back of the trailer so she could at least catch a glimpse of her.

Susan's next words stopped her cold in her tracks. "Well, J.C., I'm sorry, but this *is* a children's camp. As much as I appreciate Mr. Moncrief's offer, I'm afraid we're going to have to turn her down. We just do not have the facilities—nor the time needed to work with a wild horse."

"Now ma'am, I wouldn't say she's exactly wild. Just not too used to people yet. She's a smart one, she is. She'll tame down quick." Pausing for a moment, he looked down in discomfort. "Anyways, I can't rightly take her back with me. I have orders to pick up two more horses in the morning that the boss wants me to haul back to Texas. I'm sorry, ma'am, but I'll have to unload this little girl here. You won't be sorry if you take her. She's gonna be a good one."

"But I have nowhere..."

Kelly spoke up eagerly. "What about the rodeo and show arena? It's big and the sides are tall. We could put her in there just until she calms down. Then we could turn her into the small paddock in back of the hay barn. It's not being used right now."

Susan looked at Kelly as if she were surprised to find her still there. Sighing in defeat, she said to J.C., "I guess we have no choice. Like it or not, we have a wild horse. Let's get in the truck, and I'll direct you to where you can unload this little spitfire you have brought us."

The look of relief on his face was almost comical. It was obvious J.C. did not want to have to explain to his boss why these people had turned down his gift.

Pulling up to the large arena, J.C.'s face brightened. "Now this is more like it. She'll have plenty of room to get out her kinks, and I'll be mighty surprised if this doesn't keep her in."

"You're not the only one, J.C." Susan's dry remark brought a gleam of laughter to his eyes, but he focused his attention on backing the trailer up to the corral.

Opening the door of the truck, Kelly jumped out lightly and ran around to swing open the corral gate. Craning to catch her first glimpse of the new horse, she was disappointed to discover that the rear door of the trailer was too high for her to see over.

Once the trailer was placed so the filly could not escape from the arena around the sides, J.C. brought the truck to a halt, and he and Susan jumped out.

"How can we just let her free? I really think we should have some way to take off the traveling blanket and leg wraps before we let her go."

J.C. gave an abrupt laugh at Susan's statement. "Don't need to worry none about that. We made an attempt to dress her up for the trip, but she didn't want to have nothing to do with it. I reckon it's a good thing. Probably would have torn them all to shreds by now. But the little girl was fine. Mr. Moncrief has the best padded trailers in the business. She didn't stand a chance of getting hurt in this rig."

The concern on Susan's face deepened at the prospect of having this kind of horse at Camp Sonshine. She had agreed, however, to at least keep the horse for a few days, so she didn't say anything.

"Kelly, step back from the trailer until this girl is out." Susan's command was firm. "There's no telling how she'll come out of this trailer. She sounds mighty anxious to be free, and I don't want you getting hurt. If I'd known this is what we would be getting into, I would have sent you on up to dinner."

Kelly stepped away, but climbed up onto the fence so she could get a good view. She was thrilled to be here to experience this.

J.C. reached in through the side door to unhook the filly's lead rope and then moved quickly around back to open the doors. The second they began to swing open, the horse pushed them wide and exploded into the arena.

Crystal! Kelly could hardly believe her eyes. If she hadn't been holding on tight to the fence, she might have fallen into the arena. The wild filly was her dream horse in the flesh. Gripping the fence tighter, Kelly leaned forward and feasted her eyes. Obviously frightened, the large, coal-black filly stood with widely spaced legs and flaring nostrils. The whites of her eyes stood out against her black face as her eyes rolled in terror. *Where had this man brought her?* the filly seemed to be thinking. She looked around for the old familiar range and the friends she had grown up with but saw instead a high wooden fence and a tiny body sitting on top of it. Whirling around, she came face-to-face with the metal contraption that had brought her here, and there was another strange human beside it. The filly had had enough. Snorting in fear and confusion at her new surroundings, she reared high and came down at a dead run.

Never had Kelly seen a horse run like this one. She seemed to almost float across the wide arena. The filly's head was raised high, and her tail streamed

behind her like a banner. As she raced for the end of
the arena, Kelly had a wild thought that she was
going to jump it. At just the last moment, the filly
swerved and raced back up the middle. As she
caught sight of the things she had been running
from in the first place, she stopped short, turned on
her haunches, and took off again.

For twenty minutes the terrified horse executed
bucks and twists and turns that took Kelly's breath
away. Finally she crow-hopped to a stop at the end of
the arena and with head high, snorted her defiance.
And that's where she stayed. She couldn't get out of
this wooden prison, so she decided to stay as far as
possible from everything she feared.

Kelly let her breath out slowly. *Crystal.* For Kelly,
it was love at first sight. Already her head was full of
dreams of riding this beautiful creature—of sailing
over jumps, of racing Greg and Shandy across the
field . . .

"Well!"

Susan's voice startled Kelly out of her dreams.
With a start she realized that J.C. had left with the
truck and trailer. Kelly had not taken her eyes from
the horse since the filly had exploded from her
prison.

"I admit that I didn't know what to expect, but in
my wildest dreams I hadn't imagined this black
dynamo here. What in the world are we going to do
with her? I don't have time to tame a wild horse.
Maybe our horse trader could find someone to take
her."

Kelly turned to Susan with her eyes wide. "Oh,
please don't send Crystal away. She's just frightened. She'll calm down. I'll work with her, Susan.

I'll use all my free time and evenings as well. I'll make sure she doesn't cause any trouble."

"Crystal?"

With a flush, Kelly realized she had called the filly by name. She lowered her head and shuffled her boots around for a second before she looked Susan steadily in the eyes. "Yeah, well you see, this filly looks just like the horse I've dreamed about for so long. She's big and black, and boy is she fast. I know I can make friends with her, if you'll just give me the chance."

Susan gave her a thoughtful look and turned to watch the filly who had stopped her restless pacing but was still hiding at the end of the arena. The horse was still nervous, but her initial blind terror had subsided. Swinging back around to Kelly, Susan gazed at her in deep consideration. Kelly met her gaze with a look full of desperate confidence.

Nothing was said for several minutes. Kelly could only hold her breath and wait for Susan's decision. Susan swung her eyes back to the filly for several moments, and then nodded her head as she made her decision. "I'm probably crazy, but I'm going to let you give it a try."

Her words were cut short as Kelly gave a cry of delight and exuberantly enveloped her in a hug. "Thanks, Susan! I'll do a good job with her. You'll see."

Susan responded with a hug of her own, but then fixed Kelly with a serious look. "Yes, I'll see. I'm going to keep a close eye on you two. If I see any signs that this filly is dangerous, she goes. I'm letting you do this because I think it will be good for you. You have a natural way with horses, and you should have the chance to develop it. But remember what I've said. Just one sign that this horse is dangerous and she goes. Understand?"

Shivering with excitement, Kelly could only nod her head. Crystal couldn't be dangerous. She was Kelly's dream horse. Time would show everyone what a wonderful horse she was. Thoughts whirling, Kelly turned back around to look at the now-quiet filly. Crystal had run out all of her energy, and now her eyes just registered a fear and confusion that tore at Kelly's heart. She would win the black beauty over. The fear and confusion would be replaced with trust and confidence.

"And by the way, I think Crystal is a good name for her." Susan smiled. "From now on, Crystal she is. Now let's go get something to eat. I know you could probably care less about food right now, but you have to eat. And Crystal could use a few minutes alone to get her bearings. She'll be here when you get back. I imagine I can tell everyone not to expect you for water volleyball tonight?"

Kelly laughed at Susan's mischievous voice and nodded her agreement. "That's right. I want to be here with her the first night. Coming so far to a new place must really be scary."

"You're welcome to come back down here, but I want you to promise you won't go into the arena with her tonight. And I want you back at the cabin in time for Bible study."

"Okay. Thanks again for giving me the chance to work with her."

Susan's response was a quick hug as they walked into the now-empty dining hall. Susan was as good as her word. At her request, Dennis filled their plates with still-warm leftovers. Kelly's mind whirled as she crammed in the hamburgers, chips, and baked beans that had been tonight's meal. Susan was talking to her, but later she was unable to remember a thing she had said. Her mind was in the arena with a big, black, and scared filly named Crystal.

FOURTEEN

Reaching under her pillow to shut off her watch alarm, Kelly held her breath. Had anyone else heard the faint beeping noise? Susan and the rest of the cabin would think she was crazy to get up at five just to go check on a horse. Actually, Kelly wasn't too concerned about what everyone thought. She just didn't want to talk to Susan this morning. The head wrangler had made her promise last night that she wouldn't go in the arena with Crystal, but that was last night and this morning was now. She wouldn't be breaking a promise—not exactly, anyway.

Kelly just had to get into the arena where Crystal was. Last night she had hung on the corral until it was too dark to pick the big, black filly out from the shadows. She hadn't actually touched her, but after about an hour Crystal had moved closer to the fence. It was as if Kelly's crooning voice made her feel safer and more secure. Crystal seemed to relax as time went on, but her head would shoot up and her ears would stand erect whenever she detected a strange noise or movement. Greg had stopped by the corral

159

after he had asked Susan about Kelly's whereabouts. His admiration for the filly was obvious, but after just a few minutes he left Kelly to herself. As captain of his water volleyball team, his presence at the game was required. And as much as she enjoyed Greg's company, Kelly had been glad to be left alone on the first night with her dream horse.

Picking her way through the dark shadows created by the tall oaks surrounding her cabin, Kelly emerged into the fresh morning. With thankfulness she hugged her denim jacket closer to her body. Even in June, early mornings in the North Carolina mountains could be chilly, and she was grateful for the additional warmth. The sky was just beginning to lighten, and the last stars were fading away, but it would still be a good hour before the sun would pop over the horizon. It would also be a good hour before the early-morning crew would be down to the barn to take care of the morning feeding. This was not Kelly's morning to feed, so she would have a full two-and-a-half hours with Crystal before the breakfast gong would ring. In that amount of time, all kinds of things could happen.

Whistling a nameless tune, Kelly strode toward the rodeo arena. Stopping for just a few minutes at the barn, she stuffed handfuls of grain in each pocket of her jacket and crammed a couple of carrots into the pockets of her jeans. There was no way of knowing how familiar Crystal would be with grain and carrots since she had just come from the range, but Kelly wanted to be prepared.

"Good morning, Crystal. I see you helped yourself to some of the water and hay I left you last night.

That's a good girl. You'll soon find out this place isn't so bad after all. You and I are going to be good friends, you beautiful little girl." Keeping her voice low and steady, Kelly approached the arena gate slowly. Taking a deep breath to steady her nerves, she unlatched the gate and slipped in quickly, making sure to latch it securely behind her. Moving in just a few feet, she came to a standstill.

Crystal had flung her head up at Kelly's approach, but the terror was gone from her eyes, and she remained still. She seemed to remember Kelly. "That's right, it's me. I was here last night for you." Kelly's voice was soothing. "You're probably very confused about all that has happened in the last few weeks. One minute you're roaming across thousands of acres with your childhood friends, and the next you're being herded into a large corral with dozens of shouting men and clouds of choking dust. Then you're separated from all of your buddies and loaded into a large blue trailer. It had to have been scary, Crystal. But I'm glad they brought you here."

As Kelly's easy, crooning words filled the early-morning air, Crystal moved to within a couple of yards of where she stood. The horse came to a halt and regarded the girl with great curiosity.

"That's right, girl. You can trust me. I won't hurt you. I just want to be your friend." Kelly's entire body was shaking from excitement, but she concentrated on keeping the tremor out of her voice. Her dream horse was actually coming to her. "Come on now, Crystal. I have something for you. Don't you want to know what it is?" Continuing to talk to her in the same easy tones, Kelly stood rock still. She didn't want to seem to be going after Crystal. She wanted Crystal to come to her. She would wait as long as she had to.

In the distance she could hear the doors of the barn being swung opened and latched back. The early-morning feed team had arrived at the barn. The clang of empty feed cans filled the air, and soon she could hear the horses squealing and snorting as they vied for first place in line. It was easy to envision the rush of the horses as the gates swung back to allow them access to their stalls and the feed buckets within.

As the sounds of the early-morning activity filled the air, Crystal swung her head around and pricked her ears forward as if trying to understand the commotion. She stood that way for several minutes, and then swung her attention back to Kelly who was continuing to talk in easy tones. Her eyes reflected loneliness and confusion. Kelly's heart went out to her. Still she didn't move. Crystal must come to her.

Slowly, ever so slowly, Crystal began to move toward Kelly. Their eyes were locked and time seemed to stand still. Kelly held her breath, afraid even the slightest movement would frighten Crystal into flight. The filly hesitated several times, but her mind seemed made up. Her black body was tensed, ready for flight if need be, and her ears were pitched forward to catch the slightest hint of danger, but she continued to lessen the space between them. Taking the final step, Crystal came to a halt just in front of where Kelly stood waiting for her.

"Good girl, Crystal. I told you we would be good friends. I promise I won't hurt you." Kelly's eyes brimmed with tears as she took in her dream horse. For several minutes they stood that way, neither one making a move. Willing trust into the uncertain filly, Kelly slowly reached out her hand toward the shiny, black neck. Crystal tensed but stood still and continued to watch the girl. Gently Kelly touched the satiny skin and then, as Crystal didn't move, began to gently stroke it.

Gradually the filly's eyes softened and her tense body relaxed. Lowering her head to accept Kelly's caressing, she nickered a soft greeting.

"Oh, you beautiful thing! There is so much we're going to do together. You just wait. We'll show everyone at Camp Sonshine what a wonder horse you are." Kelly's voice trembled with the excitement welling up in her. Crystal trusted her! She could hardly believe this was the same horse that had exploded off the trailer last night in black fury and terror. She shuddered at the thought that Crystal would have been sent back on that same trailer if she hadn't been there to talk Susan into keeping her. In a daze of happiness, Kelly continued to stroke and murmur to the filly in loving words.

"I had a feeling that I would find you here!"

Crystal's head shot up at the unfamiliar voice, and some of the terror began to creep back into her eyes. Her black body tensed for flight as she searched the morning for the source of the voice.

Moving into view at the arena gate, Susan continued sternly, "I thought I told you to stay away from that horse, Kelly." The clanging of the latch being undone was more than Crystal could take. Snorting her fear, she wheeled and took off for the other end of the arena, leaving Kelly to face the angry wrangler on her own.

Casting a longing look toward the frightened filly, Kelly turned toward her indignant boss. "That was last night, Susan. You didn't actually say that I couldn't get near her this morning." Not giving Susan time to reply, Kelly rushed on. "Did you see her? She was letting me touch her. She came to me on her own. I didn't go to her. I wanted to let her know she could trust me. Oh Susan, she's not mean. She's just scared and confused and wants a friend. She won't hurt me—I know she won't! Please don't be mad. I just had to be near her. She's everything I ever imagined a horse could be." Her anxious words tumbled to an end, and she waited anxiously for Susan's reply.

Almost as though against her will, the anger faded from Susan's face and was replaced with understanding. Giving a helpless little laugh, she said, "I know I should let you have it, but somehow I just can't. The sight of you in here alone with that black beast almost made my heart stop, but it's obvious she wasn't hurting you. Did you say she came to you on her own?"

"That's right! It took a while, but she came. She needs a friend, Susan, and I want to be that friend. Please tell me that I can work with her! I'll use my time off during the day. I promise it won't affect my work. She's a wonderful horse. I'll prove it to you. She isn't wild. She just needs time to get used to everything. Please?"

Looking closely at the girl's face, Susan seemed to be considering more than just the issue of the horse.

Coming to a decision, Susan gave Kelly's shoulders a squeeze. "Okay, my little horse tamer. I for sure don't have time to do anything with her, so she's all yours. Come to me if you have any questions, and I'll do what I can to help." Pausing for a moment, she looked deep into Kelly's blue eyes. "You know, your letting Crystal trust you enough to come to you on her own is exactly what Jesus is doing for you. He wants you to trust him enough to come to him on your own. Think about it."

Kelly heard the words, but her mind was too full of Crystal to concentrate on them. As Susan walked away, Kelly turned toward the end of the arena and began to move slowly toward her dream horse.

• • •

From that day on, Kelly's life fell into a wonderful, predictable pattern. Up before anyone else, she would spend precious moments with Crystal before the rest of the camp was alive.

Other than a snort of protest, it had been a snap to introduce the halter to Crystal. Within minutes, she was willingly being led. It was a snap for Kelly, that was. Crystal was eager to do anything her young friend asked, but her attitude was one of suspicion when anyone else came near. None of the other wranglers bothered with her, and Crystal seemed to tolerate Greg only because Kelly so obviously liked him. She was willing to be handled by Susan but showed none of the eagerness she showed Kelly. Susan had laughingly told Kelly that she certainly had herself a "one-woman horse." Susan had laughed, but Kelly had detected a concern in her eyes. What would Susan do with this horse when Kelly went home?

Kelly had the answer to that. Crystal would go home with her. Kelly didn't know how much the camp would want, but with her dad's money combined with hers, she could surely buy the horse. Kelly had written a glowing letter home all about Crystal. Dad had responded with a letter of his own, urging her to be careful but to have fun. Good old Dad! Kelly thought. He probably knew what was in her mind.

"Good morning, girl!" Kelly unlatched the door and slipped into the stall that Crystal now considered home. Free to roam the large paddock behind the hay barn during the day, she was confined to the stall at night. Susan thought it best to not turn her out with the other horses yet. That was fine with Kelly because it made spending time with her easier.

Crystal nickered a glad greeting and impatiently nosed the girl's pockets, searching for the carrot that she knew Kelly carried. "Okay, okay!" Kelly laughed as she handed over the golden treasure. "Sometimes I don't know if you love me, or if you just love my carrots."

Once the carrot was consumed, Crystal nickered another soft greeting and laid her head on Kelly's shoulder. Wrapping her arms around the black filly's glistening neck, Kelly stood for a minute, allowing the wonder of her horse to convince her it was all real. Sometimes Kelly was afraid it was a dream, and she would wake up to discover she had imagined it all. Moments like these with Crystal's warm breath ruffling her hair convinced her it was real.

Stepping out of the stall, she scooped Crystal's morning grain ration into an empty can and grabbed the box of grooming implements. Retracing her steps, she dumped the can of grain into the empty feed box. Crystal buried her nose eagerly into the feed while Kelly began the morning grooming ritual. Crystal arched her back in pleasure as Kelly worked her over with the rubber currycomb. Once that was completed, Kelly used a stiff bristle brush to coax any dirt from the gleaming coat and then added an even more brilliant shine with the soft brush. Working carefully to make sure she didn't break off any hairs, she used her fingers to separate the mane and tail hairs and remove any tangles. She was still careful around Crystal's feet but instinctively knew she could trust the filly. What had started as a friendship had developed into a deep love between the two.

Putting the brushes aside, Kelly reached for the hoof pick. Running her hand down Crystal's leg, she waited until the filly lifted it for her willingly. She had been careful not to demand anything of the filly. She asked and then waited until Crystal did it. This method had deepened the trust between them. Taking the offered hoof, Kelly cleaned it carefully and then applied ointment. When Crystal had first arrived, her feet had been dried and cracked. Careful trimming and repeated application of the ointment had restored them to a strong, supple condition.

As Kelly stepped back to view her work, she said a silent word of thanks to Susan. Susan had left her alone to work with the filly, but much of Kelly's success was directly due to the wisdom and answers that Susan had provided. Susan had plenty of experience and was glad to help Kelly. The times they spent together in conversation had drawn them close together.

"Good morning, early bird!"

Crystal raised her head and snorted but showed no alarm at the sight of Greg hanging over the stall door. He often came by, whether in the mornings or in the evenings, when Kelly was spending time with her filly. Greg seemed to accept the fact that if he wanted to see Kelly, he would have to come to the barn. They spent long hours talking about any and everything. If Kelly was missing out on most of the fun the other wranglers were having, she didn't notice. Her life was full. She was content and happy. The problems of home seemed far away.

"What gets you up so early this morning?" Kelly opened the door and slipped out to join him. Crystal had finished eating and stuck her head over the door as if she, too, were interested in his answer.

"Susan slipped me the word you were going to put a saddle on this beast this morning, and I didn't want to miss it. I guess she'll be here in a minute."

Kelly nodded with excitement, coupled with a degree of nervousness. "Susan figures it's time Crystal got introduced to it. Crystal has been so good about everything I have asked of her, but this will be a big step. I hope she doesn't go crazy."

Greg grinned. "Oh, I don't know. This 'wild horse' has been acting awful tame. I wouldn't mind some honest-to-goodness bronc action." He dodged as Kelly swung at him playfully. "Seriously, though, I think this little girl will do anything for you. I doubt you'll have a problem. I just wanted to be here to see it. I still remember the first time I put a saddle on Shandy. I was on top of the world. It meant that soon I would be riding him."

At the mention of riding Crystal, Kelly's face registered both excitement and nervousness. "She's come so far in just three weeks. I can hardly believe she's the same dynamo that exploded off the truck when J.C. brought her from Texas."

"You've done a really good job with her."

Kelly blushed at Greg's compliment, but was obviously pleased. "Thanks. I have to admit, I'm kinda scared, though. What if she really blows up when I put the saddle on? Susan said she had to go if there was even a hint she was dangerous."

Greg laughed. "There isn't a dangerous bone in this horse's body!" Crystal raised her head and snorted her agreement. Her eyes were bright as if she knew what was coming and thought it was high time. "You just take it slow and easy with her. She won't let you down."

As Greg reached over to stroke Crystal's nose, Susan strode into the barn. "Sorry I'm late. I had a hard time getting this body to move when the alarm went off." She glanced in Crystal's stall. "I see she's all done with breakfast. You've finished making her beautiful, so we may as well get started. I've told you everything I know, and I don't think you'll have any problem. She seems willing to do anything you ask. I just wanted to be here if there *should* be a problem."

Taking Greg by the arm, Susan walked over to the feed bin. Offering him the box she held tucked under her arm, she seated herself and said, "I brought some doughnuts that Dennis had just pulled out of the deep fry. Didn't see any reason for us to starve while we were being entertained." Greg's face lit up with a good-natured grin, and he settled down on the feed bin with an air of anticipation.

Kelly slipped back into Crystal's stall and hid her face in her warm neck for just a moment. "Please be good, girl. I want everyone to know what a wonderful horse you are. If you act too crazy, Dad might not want me to have you for my own." Her last words were whispered for just her and the filly to hear. No one knew yet of her determined desire to make Crystal her own by the end of the summer. Once she had actually ridden her, she would then tell Susan what she wanted to do.

Snapping the lead line onto the filly's halter, she led her out into the corridor. The area was large and the ceiling was high enough so Crystal wouldn't hit her head if she reared. Susan had decided the filly's first saddling lesson was to be done in the barn. Snapping her to the cross-ties, Kelly ran the soft brush over Crystal's body one more time. The big, black filly seemed to know something new was in the air, and Kelly wanted her to relax—although she had to admit she was more nervous than the filly. Crystal just seemed eager to get on with whatever was coming.

Picking up the soft white pad that was resting on the saddle horse nearby, Kelly walked slowly over to the filly's head. Holding it firmly, she lifted it up for

Crystal's inspection. Stretching her nose out, Crystal snorted softly but showed no fear. Kelly had made sure that Crystal had seen the white pad every morning for three weeks. She had wanted to assure Crystal that it posed no threat. Crystal offered no objection when Kelly laid it gently on her back, other than to turn her head to get a closer look.

"What a good girl, Crystal." Kelly kept up an end-less stream of soothing conversation as she worked with the filly. Secretly she wanted to laugh. Susan and Greg had come down for free entertainment, but this was no harder than saddling one of the class horses. She was so proud of her beautiful filly, she could feel her heart exploding. The barn was quiet except for her murmuring. Susan and Greg were letting her handle it on her own.

Picking up the saddle, Kelly raised it, as she had the pad, for Crystal's inspection. Again the horse showed no alarm—just a mild curiosity. Sliding around to the filly's side, Kelly lifted the saddle and allowed it to settle on the horse's back. Crystal gave a snort and began to move to the side, but Kelly's voice stopped her. Crystal stood, as if uncertain of her next move. Kelly's voice never stopped flowing. With the free hand that was not holding the saddle, she reached out to stroke the silky neck, convincing her that the saddle would not hurt her. Crystal relaxed and turned her head to inspect it more closely.

"Good girl!" Kelly took just a moment to glance over at her spectators. It was obvious from the ex-pressions on their faces that they were pleased and impressed.

Things continued smoothly from there. Crystal offered no more than a token objection when the girth was loosely cinched. The tightening would occur over a few days to get her accustomed to it gradually. Even when Kelly unsnapped the cross-ties and led her out into the paddock, she gave no trouble.

"I know this is strange, girl," Kelly softly told the filly, "but you can trust me. Good things are ahead for us."

Crystal gave Kelly a look that seemed to say if Kelly wanted her to do it, she would put up with it and try to understand why.

F I F T E E N

Little puffs of dirt rose in response to the dancing hooves of the waiting, impatient horses. Kelly spoke soothingly to Samson then turned her attention to the action swirling around her. The camp rodeo never ceased to thrill her with its excitement, action, and color. It may not be a big-time operation, but it was fun, and she loved every minute of it.

All the horses had been groomed by eager campers, anxious to have the horses look their best for the events. The top board of the tall rodeo corral was lined with parents, family, and friends who had come to view the campers' biggest moment. The staff was all dressed in bright colors, resplendent in the Western wear they wore to give the rodeo a flavor of authenticity. A large, colorful tent had been erected close to the gate of the corral. It was crowded with people seeking to quench their thirst with the cool lemonade being sold. Country music blared from the large speakers stationed on top of the announcer's platform where the camp director, Randy, waited to emcee the coming event. The air was full of fun and laughter. Kelly knew that the campers would carry away a wonderful last memory of their stay at Camp Sonshine.

Finally, the music the wranglers were waiting for flowed from the speakers. Counselors and other staff members herded people to their places on the fence, and the crowd fell silent in anticipation. Kelly's heart began to beat faster, and she took a firmer grip on Samson's reins. The opening strains of the grand entry never failed to elicit this response from her. Glancing over at Tina, she saw the same anticipation mirrored on her friend's face. The wranglers as a whole group practiced two mornings a week for this very moment, but anything could happen. One moment of bad timing, and the whole pattern could be destroyed, or worse, there could be a collision between the horses.

Tina glanced her way and grinned, "Here goes nothing. This is fun, but it sure is nerve-wracking."

Kelly nodded her agreement as the chord they were awaiting was played. As one, the whole group urged their mounts into a full run and burst into the arena to the cheers of the crowd. Not that Kelly heard any of the noise. Her full attention was on the maneuvers that she was to execute. In a double-breasted line they surged down the center of the arena. Each pair of wranglers was mounted on almost matching horses, and their colorful shirts were identical. Approaching the end of the arena, Kelly tightened her grip on Samson as they loomed upon the gate. At the last possible moment, she swung the big bay to the right as Tina swung her mount left. The remaining pairs of wranglers followed their movements. Halfway down the arena

Kelly gave Samson his signal. He swung back toward the center of the arena just as Tina and her mount did. Checking Samson just a little, she waited until Tina had crossed the center of the arena and then urged him forward so that his head crossed just as the hindquarters of Tina's mount passed. The rest of the wranglers followed them in the crisscross pattern. Glancing back, Kelly noticed with relief that everyone was in proper position. Racing down to the end of the arena, she counted the seconds and at just the right moment swung Samson around to race back up the arena. Tina was executing the same move. Their stirrups almost met as side by side they surged up the center of the arena. Kelly was only vaguely aware of the shouts of approval from the crowd. She allowed herself a brief grin at Tina. She knew that behind them, as the last pair of wranglers headed up the center, Susan would race through the gate, carrying a huge American flag. Checking Samson's speed to a controlled canter, she and Tina moved a little apart. Seconds later, Susan tore between them, with the flag flapping in full glory.

Just beyond the center of the arena, Susan pulled her horse to an abrupt stop. Moving farther apart from each other, Kelly and Tina brought their horses to a stop several feet from the lead horse's hindquarters. Spreading out to form an arrow, the remaining wranglers fell into formation. With the last strain of music dying on the air, a reverent silence fell over the crowd.

With the close of the grand entry came the opening bars of the national anthem. Everyone came to attention as Susan urged her mount into a full run

and circled the arena. It was a sight that never failed
to raise strong emotions in Kelly. The flying flag
along with the beautiful music that blared from the
speakers filled her with pride for her country. She
was glad to be an American.

Having completed her circuit, Susan came riding
up through the arrow and repositioned herself at
the front. Randy, the camp director, then led the
whole crowd in the Pledge of Allegiance.

Silence fell once more and, at a signal from
Susan, the departing formation began. Susan urged
her horse to a canter, and Kelly fell in right behind
her. One by one they all formed a single-file line
and, at a run, moved from the rodeo arena. The
applause of an enthusiastic crowd followed them.
Once they were out, they allowed themselves only a
few moments of congratulation for a job well done.
Their real work was about to begin.

For the next two hours clouds of dust rose from
the arena along with the squeals and cries of enthusiastic campers. It was hectic, but things ran smoothly
as the wrangling staff sent the campers through the
organized events. The key-hole race and potato
race were for beginners, while the intermediate
riders were challenged with the ribbon race and
running the poles. Advanced riders enjoyed the
thrills of running the barrels and the frustration of
trying to capture as many rings as possible in the
ring race.

Kelly's favorite event was last on the agenda. The
crew worked swiftly to remove all of the props
needed for the Western events, and then speedily set
up the jumps for Kelly's English riders. There were

only four of them this week, but they were all looking to Kelly for encouragement. "Okay, everybody!" Kelly said enthusiastically. "Let's go out there and show them what we can do. Remember, if I didn't know you could do this, I wouldn't have you doing it. You've all come a long way. I'm proud of you, and your parents will be, too!" Looking at the serious faces surrounding her, she grinned lightly. "Just remember to keep those heels and hands down, and keep your seat out of the saddle. Your horse will do the rest."

Kelly watched in pride as all of her students successfully completed the course she had set up for them. There was only one anxious moment, when Fair Warning, a large sorrel mare, refused a jump. Her young rider, however, refused to be beaten. She circled her and came at it again. This time the mare went over it smoothly. The crowd applauded her persistence, and she rode in with a glowing face.

The rest of the morning passed in a blur as Kelly exchanged hugs and addresses with the young campers who promised to write and to never forget her. Feeling someone take her arm she turned, expecting to look down on another little camper. Instead, she had to look up and into the laughing eyes of Greg. "If you're done with your admiration society, do you think we could have some lunch? I'm starving!"

"You looked like you had your own admiration society over there yourself. Especially the girls!" Kelly tossed her retort at him with a grin as she took his proffered arm.

"Do I detect a note of jealousy?"

"Woe unto me if I have to be jealous of a crowd of nine- and ten-year-olds! Besides, as far as I know, you're a free agent." Kelly tossed the last words out deliberately to see what response they would evoke.

"That could change any day, you know. Anyway, most people up here don't see me as a free agent." His good-natured response brought a flush to her already-hot cheeks. She was saved from a response by Tina.

"Hey, Kelly," Tina called as she walked up, "isn't today your day to finally ride Crystal?"

With the rodeo behind her, Kelly could allow herself to think of something else. The upcoming events of the afternoon filled her with breathless anticipation. "It is. I can hardly believe it's finally here. Susan seems to think it's time. Crystal is used to the saddle and bridle, and I've been ground training her for two weeks now. Susan says she's the fastest learner she's ever seen. I can hardly wait to sit on her back."

Tina was obviously impressed, but she was also a little skeptical. "Aren't you afraid she'll throw you? After all, she was a wild horse just weeks ago."

Kelly tried to shrug nonchalantly. "Well, I guess there is always that chance, but I'm willing to take it. Crystal seems eager to do anything I ask of her. Susan doesn't think she'll give me much of a fight, if any at all, but time will tell." Quickening her steps, she headed for the dining hall. "Right now I just want to get lunch out of the way."

With all the campers gone, the dining hall felt very empty. Kelly was glad for the tranquillity after such a busy week. Filling their trays, she and Greg moved over to sit beside Susan. Susan looked up with a smile, and then said in a voice loud enough for everyone to hear, "That was a great job with the rodeo this morning. Y'all make it look almost easy to push more than a hundred kids through all their events in just two hours. I've never worked with a better group of wranglers."

A chorus of thanks rose around them as Kelly and Greg settled down. Susan turned to Kelly and smiled warmly. "So today's the big day, huh? Are you excited?" She laughed at Kelly's look. "Okay, so I didn't need to ask." Taking a bite of her lasagna, Susan hastily chewed and swallowed it. "By the way," she said, "I made that phone call we were talking about the other day."

Kelly stopped eating and looked up with great interest. "And..." She knew what Susan was referring to. Ever since Crystal had arrived, Susan insisted she was more than two years old—that her teeth and size spoke of her being at least three. That was important. Susan didn't believe in riding a two-year-old. She thought they needed more time for their bones and muscles to become strong and solid before they accepted the added pressure of a human on their back. Susan had seen too many horses who had been pushed before they were ready. The result had been bad legs and sour attitudes. But Susan had been sure that Crystal was older.

"I was right." Susan grinned. "I talked to Mr. Moncrief. He said that somehow Crystal managed to escape the roundup last year. His men saw her take off through the brush but didn't have the time to go after her. Their hands were too full with the others in the corral. Anyway, they were able to get her this year. Mr. Moncrief said the extra year on the range had been wonderful for her—that she was the strongest, most well-built filly he had seen in a long time. And he told me to tell you congratulations on your fine work and asked if you might be willing to come down and help him with the rest."

Kelly blushed at the compliment and sat back with a sigh of relief. Even though Susan had been so sure Crystal was older than they thought, Kelly had still been afraid she might ask too much of her before she was ready. But now she knew for sure she was three years old. It wouldn't hurt Crystal to be ridden. Kelly finished her meal with dreams of the hours she and Crystal would spend exploring the countryside.

• • •

Kelly was especially careful when she went down to the barn to tack Crystal up. She laid the saddle pad on the filly's back several times before she was satisfied that it was perfectly smooth and that there were no hairs pressed the wrong direction that could cause any irritation. Hauling the Western saddle from the saddle horse, she placed it carefully on Crystal's back. Susan had suggested a Western saddle. If Crystal should decide to buck, there would be a lot more to hold on to. Kelly had made sure the filly was as familiar with a Western saddle as she was with the lighter, smaller, English version. She was careful to tuck the pad up into the pommel of the saddle so it wouldn't rub Crystal's withers and cause any sores. It was important her first experience be a positive one.

Satisfied that the saddle was correct, Kelly turned to the bridle. Susan and she had been in agreement that the only thing they would ever use in Crystal's mouth was a jointed snaffle. They knew such a bit, as long as the rider had good hands, would never punish Crystal's mouth. Crystal had responded well to it over the last couple of weeks of ground training. Susan insisted it was a mark of a well-trained, obedient horse.

Finally, there was no more to do to prepare for the big moment. Kelly led the filly from the barn just as Susan and Greg strolled up. After close inspection, Susan nodded her approval and said with a grin, "The rest of the crew wanted to come down, but I persuaded them to take a dip in the pool instead. I didn't figure you would be too interested in an audience for your first time, and I didn't want anything to upset Crystal."

"You're right. I want this first time to be just us. Thanks!"

Crystal chose that moment to begin to dance nervously. Turning all her attention to the black filly by her side, Kelly spoke to her soothingly, "It's all right, girl. Take it easy now." Pricking up her ears to catch the soothing voice, Crystal calmed down but her eyes were bright with curiosity. She seemed to know this was a big day. Neck arched, she pranced lightly at Kelly's side as they headed for the big rodeo arena that would be the site of the landmark experience.

Though Kelly's hands were busy with the filly, she was aware of the beautiful day for the event. A terrific thunderstorm the night before had cleaned the air and brightened everything with a fresh splash of color. The sky was a deep, clear blue, and there were just enough puffy clouds to decorate the painter's canvas. The leaves of the trees tossed about in a bright circus of green hues, and the color of flitting birds contrasted sharply. The sparkling air even seemed to bring an added sheen to Crystal's already brilliant black coat. As she pranced at Kelly's side, it was obvious she felt wonderful.

As they moved to the arena, Greg walked up to Kelly's side and smiled at her sober face. "I remember the day I first rode Shandy. Boy, was I excited—and nervous. He was the first horse I had trained all by myself, and I wanted everyone to be as proud of him as I was. Plus, I knew I'd die of embarrassment if he dumped me."

Kelly flashed him a silent look of gratitude for understanding. Greg always knew what to say.

"Anyway, I'm rooting for you," he added. "You've worked hard with this filly. I've never seen one learn so fast. It's just because she loves you so much. You don't have much to worry about. Just enjoy yourself."

At that moment they arrived at the gate, and Greg stepped back as Susan swung it open. Kelly noticed a tightness in Susan's shoulders that spoke of her tenseness, but none of it showed in her voice as she spoke lightly. "Okay, my cowgirl. This is your moment—although I still wonder if I'm crazy to let you try this." She laughed and her eyes regarded the girl with warmth. "I've never seen anyone love a horse more than you do Crystal, though. Once you're on top, just let her get the hang of the whole thing and go real easy. She's eager to please you. You just have to make sure she doesn't get confused." With those final words, she gave Kelly's shoulders a tight squeeze and stepped out of the corral door, latching it securely behind her.

This was it. Taking a deep breath, Kelly gathered the reins in one hand and placed her foot in the stirrup. Crystal turned to look in curiosity. This was something new. As Kelly looked in the filly's eyes she knew she saw only curiosity—not fear. The knowledge filled her with confidence. Grasping the pommel with her left hand, she sprang lightly from the ground and settled herself into the saddle. As Crystal felt the sudden weight on her back, she snorted and began to stiffen up. Holding the reins firmly but lightly, Kelly spoke to her with a soft, easy voice. Crystal flicked one ear back to indicate she was listening, but not one muscle of her body relaxed. Impatiently she shook her head, as if she was deciding what to do. For several minutes this battle of the minds went on. Kelly's smooth voice flowed into the air while the filly debated her decision.

Now that Kelly was actually on her filly's back, she was filled with confidence. The calmness of her voice was natural, not forced. Crystal was meant to be hers. She knew that the filly felt it, too. She just needed a minute to get used to it. Kelly was ready for anything, but she was trusting her horse not to give her a fight. *Her* horse. She couldn't help calling Crystal hers—at least in her own mind. She still hadn't said anything to anyone, even though she was sure Greg knew what she wanted. There would be time enough for that when she could write home that she had ridden Crystal and tell everyone what a wonderful horse she was.

Gradually Crystal relaxed under her calm voice and soothing touch. Finally she turned her head and looked at Kelly as if to inquire *why* she was sitting on her back. Kelly waited for a few more minutes, and then gave her a quiet command to walk. Crystal knew the command from all her hours of ground training. Hesitating for just a moment, she shook her head and then moved out with her ground-eating stride.

Kelly felt as if her heart would burst. She was actually riding her horse! One she had trained all on her own. At that moment she wished Mandy could see her. So many times she had told her friend about the big black filly she would own and train one day. Suddenly the whole incredible day took on an even greater brightness. Kelly felt as if anything in the world were possible.

As Crystal began to move around the ring, she tossed her head and danced a few light steps. Another quiet command from Kelly and she broke into a nice, smooth trot. Around and around they went, as if they were the only ones in the world.

Outside the gate, Susan relaxed as she viewed Kelly's obvious success. "I guess we have ourselves a real cowgirl. When I saw that black beast explode from the trailer several weeks ago, I wouldn't have given a wooden nickel that someone would be riding her now."

Greg grinned in agreement. "She's something all right. Crystal and her have got something real special—just like me and Shandy. Watching those two together makes me miss him a lot."

At that moment, they became aware of the presence of Randy, the camp director. Giving them a smile, he crossed his arms over the top of the gate and gave his whole attention to the pair circling the arena. The three observers couldn't help but notice the eager willingness of the filly and the beauty of her well-proportioned body, the fine lines of her clean legs and the easy way that her stride ate up the ground. Nodding his head, Randy turned to Susan and Greg. "Mr. Moncrief did us a big favor when he sent that beauty up. I haven't seen such a fine horse in a long time. Didn't you tell me that all her training has been done by Kelly?"

Susan spoke up proudly, "Kelly did everything. They have a natural love for each other. That filly will do anything she asks. They are quite a pair."

Randy said nothing but turned to look again at the duo in the arena.

Kelly felt that Crystal had done enough for the first time and brought her to an easy halt out in the middle of the arena. Once she had dismounted, she allowed her calm to desert her and threw her arms around the filly's neck in ecstasy. Kelly had finally ridden her horse, and she had been a dream. Crystal snorted and nudged her shoulder as if to indicate that it had been fun for her, too.

Feeling a tap on her shoulder, Kelly turned into Greg's arms. Giving her an exuberant hug and excited grin, he said, "Congratulations! I knew you could do it. Crystal will do anything for you. Nobody that didn't know would have ever guessed she's never been ridden before today."

"My turn." Smiling, Susan pushed Greg aside and gave Kelly a hug of her own. "I am so proud of you! The two of you looked like pros out there. Your love for Crystal has turned the two of you into quite a pair. I sure wish I could keep you around all year. My job would be a lot easier."

Kelly, flushed with pride and excitement, turned to give Crystal another hug. "Thanks, you guys. She did so well! To finally ride her was even more incredible than I thought. Boy, have I got plans for the rest of the summer."

And for more than just the rest of the summer. Maybe this was a good time to tell Susan of her dream to make Crystal her own, Kelly considered. Now that she had actually ridden her, no one would be afraid that Crystal was dangerous and too much for Kelly to handle. Eager words rose to her lips, and she turned to face the head wrangler.

"Excuse me. I hope you don't mind if I break in on your little party. I just wanted to congratulate you on some fine work, Kelly."

Kelly whirled toward the gate. She had no idea that someone else had been watching. "Oh hi, Randy. Thanks a lot! Crystal is some horse—beautiful and smart as a whip, too!" Kelly's thoughts whirled. The camp director had seen her ride Crystal! This *was* a good time to tell them. Surely Randy and Susan together would be able to convince her dad that Kelly could indeed handle the big filly. She couldn't believe her good fortune.

"Crystal is indeed a beautiful horse, Kelly." Randy spoke before Kelly could say a word. "And she must be every bit as smart as you say. I've never seen a horse learn as fast as this one. Susan gave me a full report when she arrived, and I must say I was concerned about letting you work with her. I can see I need not have been." Randy's voice was warm with admiration. "That brings me to the real reason I came down here today. My wife, Donna, has been after me all spring to find her a good saddle horse. I know we have several fine horses here, but none of them really strike her fancy. When she was out walking around camp the other day, she saw you with Crystal, and that's all she has talked about since. Donna's a good rider, but I wasn't sure she could handle a horse like this. After seeing what you've done with her, I feel sure that by the end of the summer you will have her ready for my wife. Keep up the good work, Kelly!" With a wave of his hand, Randy headed back to his office.

Kelly could do nothing but stare at his retreating back. She felt like she had been kicked in the stomach, and a sick feeling washed over her whole being. Her dreams lay shattered in the dust around her.

Susan's voice broke into her numbed thoughts. "Well, he paid you a real compliment. Randy is quite a horseman himself, so he recognizes quality horseflesh and talent when he sees it. You have a right to be very proud of yourself."

Kelly turned and looked at Susan's face but still couldn't bring herself to say anything. Crystal was to become Donna's horse, not hers. There would be no long hours riding with Greg and Shandy. There would be no early mornings spent in Crystal's stall, grooming her while she ate. She could forget the excitement of teaching Crystal to jump. The horse she loved with every fiber of her being was going to belong to someone else.

"Kelly, are you okay? Have the sun and excitement made you sick? You don't look so good." Susan took Kelly's shoulders and turned her so that she could see the girl's face clearly. Kelly caught a glimpse of Greg's face over Susan's shoulder. From the look on his face, she knew he felt as sick as she did. She had never told him of her plans, but she knew that he knew. His own pain and sympathy gave her a tiny bit of strength.

"I'm okay, Susan." She tried to laugh but it came out shaky. "I guess maybe the excitement *has* gotten to me. I'll be fine. Crystal has had enough for one day. I'm going to take her back to the barn. I'll join you guys at the pool later." All she wanted right then was to be alone. Greg's sympathy had given her strength, but any more of it and she would dissolve in tears.

Once in the barn and away from prying eyes, she allowed the tears to come. Sobs racked her body as she clung to Crystal's neck. Why hadn't she told Susan of her dreams? Maybe Susan could have talked to Randy before his wife decided she wanted Crystal. Now it was too late. When Kelly left at the end of the summer, she would be alone. Crystal would stay at Camp Sonshine.

At that moment, the big black filly gave a soft nicker and nudged Kelly gently with her velvety nose. When Kelly gave no response, she nudged her again, only this time harder. Still not receiving any attention, Crystal raised one perfectly formed hoof and stamped the ground.

"Okay, okay." Wiping her eyes, Kelly moved back from the horse's neck and looked into her eyes. She knew it was impossible, but Crystal seemed to be trying to say something to her. As Kelly gazed into the dark, liquid pools, a feeling of calm began to creep over her body. Summer wasn't over yet. She and Crystal still had four weeks. It wasn't long, but if that was all the time she had left with her dream horse, she'd better make the most of it.

SIXTEEN

You know, you were right," Greg admitted. "This *is* the best time of the day to ride. I'm glad you finally convinced me to drag myself out of bed this early. It's like we have the whole mountain all to ourselves. And it feels so cool. It gets so hot and muggy by late afternoon that I have to admit the pool is a lot more appealing than a ride by that time."

Kelly reined Crystal to a halt and took a deep breath of the fresh mountain air. "I love it when I can say I told you so! See what you've been missing for the last two weeks?" She tossed the words out teasingly to Greg, who was mounted on a big sorrel gelding beside her.

Kelly had determined to spend every spare minute with Crystal until the end of the summer. That included early mornings, free time during the day, and evenings. The rest of the camp staff was used to seeing her only at meals and evening Bible studies. She would have skipped those too, if it had been possible. The day before, Greg had made a joking comment about never seeing her anymore. That wasn't entirely true, but she could tell he was a little hurt. They still saw each other, but their times alone were rare. Kelly missed their times together too, but she was pushed by the knowledge that summer would soon be over and she would lose her horse. A talk with Susan had gained Kelly and Greg permission to take early-morning rides together for the rest of the summer.

Crystal arched her neck and snorted her pleasure. She seemed to love these excursions as much as Kelly. It was nothing short of amazing that she had come so far in only two weeks. The filly was responsive to Kelly's slightest touch, and every day she learned something new. They did work in the rings for an hour in the afternoons, but the mornings were spent meandering over the trails that crisscrossed the mountains above camp. There were many times that Kelly would dismount and just walk alongside Crystal. The filly seemed to never tire of hearing how much Kelly loved her.

"I guess we'd better head back," Greg broke into the quietness. "Breakfast is in about thirty minutes, and we still have to feed and groom these guys."

Kelly gave a sigh and agreed. "You're right, I suppose. Some mornings I wish I could just disappear with Crystal and never come back."

"Yeah, I know what you mean."

Kelly was grateful for Greg's understanding. She was sure he knew what she was going through, but he hadn't said much. He was letting her handle it by herself, but Kelly knew she had his full support. As the days went by, it was getting harder and harder to think of losing Crystal. The filly was so much *her* horse. How could she possibly give her up to someone else?

• • •

As the sun rose higher into the sky, the cool of the morning was forgotten. Kelly wiped the sweat from her forehead and shaded her eyes with her hand to catch a glimpse of her next class. The early mornings and long days were catching up with her. Fatigue was growing in her body. One more class and the day would be over. It would be none too soon, as far as she was concerned.

"Hi, Kelly!" Ten-year-old Megan bounded across the field and grinned up at her teacher.

"Hi, yourself! Where's the rest of the motley crew?"

"Oh, they're coming. I just wanted to get here early. I'm going to jump today for the first time, you know!"

Kelly grinned at the excited little girl. And little she was. Growing didn't seem to be something she had thought about doing. She was smaller than many of the six- and seven-year-olds at the camp. She loved horses, though, and she had worked hard for the privilege of being able to jump. Her parents were spending a month in Europe this summer, and she had begged for the opportunity to spend all that time at camp. This was her last week, and she had finally advanced to the stage where Kelly felt good about letting her go over some low jumps.

"Yep, today's the day. You've worked hard, and I know you'll do fine."

At that moment the rest of her class walked up. Most of the kids at camp rode Western, so Kelly's classes were usually small. This week was no exception. There were two other girls and one boy. They had taken lessons at home, so all of them were already jumping. Megan would join their ranks today.

"Megan sure is excited," Pam, the counselor for the ten-year-old girls, commented. "The only thing she's talked about all day is being able to jump like everyone else. Are you sure you're ready for this little ball of energy?"

"Oh, I think I'll be able to handle it." Kelly smiled. Pam always seemed to have some girls who wanted to ride English, so she and Kelly had gotten to be good friends over the summer. "Okay, everyone, mount your horses and get loosened up."

Turning around to pick up a piece of paper she had spotted, Kelly glanced over at the barn. What she saw froze her in her tracks. Susan was just leading Crystal from the barn. Walking beside her was Donna, Randy's wife. Crystal was completely tacked up, and they were headed toward the rodeo arena. Donna was going to ride *her* horse! This was the first time Donna had come down to the stable. During the last few days Kelly had allowed herself the luxury of imagining that her conversation with Randy had been a dream, but this shattered all those illusions. Crystal really was going to become Donna's horse.

Kelly's thoughts spun around. Maybe Crystal would throw Donna. That would serve her right for thinking she could steal her horse. Maybe Crystal wouldn't even let her get on. Susan had said she was a one-woman horse, and no one other than Kelly had ever ridden her. Thoughts continued to spin in her head until she was interrupted by a small voice.

"I'm ready, Kelly."

Kelly turned and looked into Megan's eager yet uncertain face. She knew the little girl had been waiting weeks for her big chance. Forcing herself to turn away from the barn, she attempted to focus her attention on her class. There was nothing she could do anyway. Crystal belonged to Camp Sonshine.

Pam was looking at her with a puzzled expression. Kelly knew her anguish and anger must be written all over her face. Forcing a lightness into her voice, she ordered her class to circle the ring at a posting trot.

The class was a disaster. Her students and even the horses seemed to sense Kelly's frustration and turmoil. Skilled at controlling their horses just the day before, the students now seemed unable to do even the simplest things. Several times Megan allowed her horse to crowd in too close to the other horses. The third time it happened, Jason, normally an even-tempered gelding, lashed out and caught Megan's horse, Sugar, square on the chest.

"Keep those horses apart!" Kelly shouted. "Someone is going to get hurt."

Flushed with embarrassment, Megan hauled back on Sugar's reins.

"Don't pull so hard on those reins. You shouldn't punish the horse for something that isn't his fault." As Kelly yelled the words, a small voice spoke in her

head, *And you shouldn't punish the children for something that isn't their fault, either.* Hot, frustrated, and
tired, she pushed the voice aside.

Striding into the center of the ring, she began to
assemble the three small jumps that made up the
jump course for her classes. The rodeo arena was on
the other side of the hay barn that stood squarely in
her path. All she could do was imagine what was
happening with her beautiful black filly. The turmoil within her grew.

"All right, Shannon. Keep Ralph at a trot and go
through the course."

The little girl's face was tight with concentration,
but try as she might she couldn't get Ralph over any
of the jumps. Usually a willing jumper, Ralph swung
around every jump as she headed him into it.

"Legs, legs! You've got to use your legs. They look
like pieces of spaghetti." Kelly usually yelled out
these words in a joking tone that kept everyone relaxed, but today she said them in anger and everyone
knew it. After several more attempts, Kelly ordered
the little girl back out on the fence. She chose to
ignore the unhappy look on Shannon's face.

Kristin, the next student to try the course, managed to get her horse to take the jumps, but Cocoa
went through them like a sluggish snail and clipped
all the jumps with her back feet. Chad's attempt was
not much better. Finally Megan's turn came. Her
face still registered excitement over the prospect of
her first jump.

"Okay, Megan. I want you to keep Knee Sox at a
steady trot and take him over the first jump. Remember
everything I told you. Keep your hands down low on

her neck and keep that seat out of the saddle. Knee Sox will do the rest."

Megan nodded her head at Kelly and screwed up her face in tight concentration. Normally Kelly would have joked with her until the little girl had loosened up, but her mind was with Crystal. Megan moved her pony into a good trot, but as she approached the jump, her legs lost their grip and Knee Sox decided to do it her way. Just a stride from the low rail, the pony came abruptly to a halt, changed her mind, and lunged over the jump. Megan, thrown totally off balance, fell back into the saddle and jerked hard on the pony's mouth. Knee Sox threw her head up in protest at the pain and knocked the rail off the jump standards with her back legs. She plowed to a stop on the other side of the jump and refused to move.

"What in the world do you think you're doing?" Kelly burst out. "You're going to tear her mouth up! If that's the best you can do, then obviously you're not ready to jump yet."

"Hey, Kelly. Go easy on her. It's obvious she's upset already."

Kelly heard Pam's quiet words as she moved out to where Megan sat on Knee Sox. She bit back her angry words when she saw the tears streaming down Megan's face. The little voice had been right. It wasn't fair to take out her anger on the kids. They hadn't done anything. Kelly forced herself to calm down and laid her hand on Megan's knee. "I'm sorry I yelled at you. I'm not feeling so good today." The horn in the distance signaled the end of class. "The first time wasn't so great, but we'll try again tomorrow. There are just a few things we need to work on. You'll get better with practice."

Megan managed a shaky smile and dismounted from the stubborn pony. Everyone seemed glad for the class to be over, and Kelly was well aware of the accusing looks Pam was sending her way.

● ● ●

Kelly was the last one to leave the barn that night. Heading toward Crystal's stall to let her out into the back paddock, she heard Susan call her name. She had wondered when it was coming. Pam had headed straight to Susan's office after class today. It didn't take much imagination to figure out what was said.

Susan was finishing up some paperwork when Kelly walked into her office. Glancing up, she nodded her head toward an empty seat, and Kelly sat down nervously. Kelly hadn't been this nervous in Susan's presence since the first interview. She had blown it, and she knew it.

Shoving the last papers into a drawer, Susan leaned forward on her desk and gazed at the distraught girl. Kelly tried to meet Susan's eyes, but her eyes wavered and fell.

"Okay, Kelly," Susan said quietly. "You want to tell me what's going on? You're my best teacher. I could hardly believe what Pam told me about your class today. What's wrong?"

Kelly had expected a tongue-lashing, not a warm, concerned person asking her what was wrong. It was so much like something her mother would have done. Her defenses crumbled before the kindness. Fighting back the tears swimming in her eyes, all Kelly could do was look at Susan.

"Let me see if I can guess. You saw me take Crystal out to the rodeo arena with Donna today. Right?" Kelly's stricken face confirmed Susan's suspicions. "Kelly, I know how much you love that black filly, but surely you knew the summer would end sometime."

The dam broke, and all of Kelly's feelings came pouring out. "But that's just it. I knew the summer would end, but I was planning on taking Crystal with me. She's the dream horse I've always wanted." Stopping for a breath, she noticed Susan's puzzled look. "I know I haven't told you that. I was waiting until I had actually ridden Crystal so no one would think she was too dangerous to be my very own. Just as I was getting ready to tell you, Randy walked up and dropped his bombshell. I have the money for her, and I know my dad would let me have her." Searching her mind frantically for the right thing to say, Kelly rushed on, "I love her, Susan. And she loves me. You said yourself that she was a one-woman horse. I'm that one woman. Crystal is meant to be with me." Her voice catching in a sob, Kelly stopped and lifted her desperate eyes to Susan.

Susan sat back in her chair with a troubled look. She spoke slowly, "I guess I should have talked to you about it. I know how much you love Crystal, but I didn't think about you having enough money to buy her. And even if I had, I don't know the camp would sell her to you. She was given as a gift by a very important supporter of the camp. Not to mention the fact Donna really likes her. I'm afraid she has her heart set on Crystal as her personal horse. I'm not really in a position to change that."

Kelly grew more heartsick as Susan spoke. Any flickering hope was being snuffed out with each word from the head wrangler. She might as well forget it. Crystal would never be hers. She had found her dream horse only to lose her.

Susan stopped speaking and silence filled the room. She stared at Kelly as if she were deciding how to continue. "Kelly, I know how hard this must be for you. You and Crystal have a very special love. I don't understand it all, but I'm sure God has a purpose in it. He loves you, and you can trust him to do what is best for you. Sometimes it's really hard to believe that, but it is always true."

Kelly felt the anger boiling up in her but was helpless to stop the flood of words that spewed from her mouth. She had heard all that she wanted to hear about how much Jesus loved her. If he loved her, then taking Crystal away from her was a lousy way to show it. "If this is the way God shows his love," Kelly boldly voiced her feelings, "I don't want to have anything to do with him. I was doing fine until everyone came along and started shoving Jesus down my throat. First Dad, then Peggy, after that Greg, and now you! This has been some kind of year. I've got a stepmother who I never asked for and who I wish I never had to see again. I've found my dream horse only to lose her after a few months. To top it all off, the only thing anyone has to say is *trust Jesus*. I'm sick of hearing his name. He hasn't done anything for me but make me miserable."

Kelly's outburst left her exhausted, and she slumped back in the seat in misery. She'd done it now. Susan would know that Kelly had lied to get the job.

Kelly looked up startled when Susan sat down next to her on the sofa. Taking Kelly's dirty hands in her own, Susan fixed her with a warm, caring look. "Kelly, I know how miserable you must be. You're not telling me anything I hadn't already guessed. I knew you weren't a Christian when you came up for the interview." She smiled at Kelly's look of astonishment and continued, "I had to pray hard about hiring you. I only gave you the job because I sensed how much you needed Jesus, and he gave me the assurance that you were to be here this summer. Kelly, your bitterness is going to hurt *you* more than anyone else. I'm sure it's already hurt your father and stepmother, but in the end it will hurt you more than anyone. You'll never be happy as long as you carry it inside of you."

Kelly's eyes were locked on her hands, and her whole body was as tense as a coiled spring. Susan released one of her hands and, taking Kelly's chin, lifted it until they were looking eye to eye. "You need Jesus. He is the only one who can release the bitterness inside of you and help you sort out your life. He loves you. You know all the words from church and Sunday school, but just knowing the words won't do you any good. You have to accept them for yourself. Remember that first morning when Crystal came to you? You said that she had to trust you enough to come to you on her own. Jesus is waiting for you to do the same thing. He'll never force you. It has to be your own decision."

For the first time, Kelly really listened. Reason battled with the anguish and confusion in her heart.

Susan gave her a warm hug. "I love you, Kelly. I just heard the dinner bell. Why don't you head on up? It's been a long time since lunch, and I'm sure you're starving. If you want to talk, just come find me."

SEVENTEEN

Kelly moved mechanically from the dim interior of the barn into the bright sunshine. Crystal nickered softly to remind her that she was still confined to the stall, but Kelly was too preoccupied to notice the sound.

Minutes later, Susan emerged from her office. She was absorbed in her own troubled thoughts and also took no notice of the black filly. Crystal stepped back into the shadows and took a big mouthful of the hay left over from lunch. At least she wasn't alone. Three other horses being treated for different illnesses had been left in for the night as well.

Kelly seemed to be on automatic pilot as she moved through the camp. It was quieter than usual. The only noise was the hum of voices and the muted clatter of silverware as everyone lined up for dinner in the dining hall. Glad that no one was around to see her so miserable, she headed toward the cabin. Dinner was out of the question. She wasn't hungry and if she had to talk to anyone, Kelly was sure what little bit of control she had left would be destroyed.

Stumbling over a rock in the path, Kelly barely managed to miss walking headlong into a tree. Shaking her head, she tried to pull herself together. Stumbling around wasn't going to do her any good. She had to get ahold of herself. Kelly searched her mind for someone she could talk to. Maybe that would help.

Dad! They hadn't talked much since he had married Peggy, but he was the only one who really understood her. Changing her course, Kelly headed toward the pay phone at the main office. He should be home from the office by now. Suddenly the most important thing in the world was hearing her father's voice. He would know how she felt.

Waiting breathlessly, Kelly listened to the ring on the other end of the phone. Closing her eyes, she could imagine her dad striding across the sun-filled kitchen. He would be wearing his white tennis shorts and one of his favorite golf shirts. His skin would be bronzed by the summer sun, and he would laugh with delight when he heard her voice. Kelly ached for her father.

"Hello?" The voice was distinctly female. And decidedly adult. Peggy!

Kelly leaned back against the wall in disappointment. "Uh—hello, Peggy. Can I speak with Dad?"

"Well, hello, Kelly. I'm sorry, but your father isn't in yet. He had a client who wanted to look at a house tonight, so he won't be in until late."

"Oh." Kelly's disappointment was obvious.

"Are you okay? Is there anything I can do for you?"

Kelly searched her mind desperately for something she could say. She wasn't prepared to carry on idle chatter, but she wasn't about to tell Peggy her problems either.

Peggy's voice was warm and concerned. "Kelly, what is it? Are you all right? You're not hurt, are you?"

Kelly forced herself to speak. "No. No, I'm not hurt. Look, I'm okay. I just wanted to talk to Dad. Just tell him I called."

Peggy's voice was more insistent this time. "Are you sure there is nothing wrong? You don't sound very happy."

Kelly responded tightly, "Look, I'm okay. I just wanted to talk to Dad. He's not there, so I'll call back later."

The concern in Peggy's voice was obvious, "Whatever you say, Kelly. I'll tell him you called and . . . I'll be praying for you."

Kelly's last shred of control slipped away. "I don't want you praying for me! All I've heard since you showed up in my life is Jesus, Jesus, Jesus. Who needs him? He hasn't done anything for me. My life was fine until you came along and ruined it. I never asked for you to marry my father. I wish I never had to see you again. I'm tired of everyone pushing religion down my throat. If it wasn't for you, I wouldn't need it anyway. I hate you. I hate you!" Her last words ended in a scream, and she slammed the phone down. Exhausted, she slumped down on the bench and buried her head in her hands.

"Well, that was certainly a pretty little speech."

Kelly jerked her head up at the sound of Greg's voice. He was eyeing her with contempt. "Did it make her highness feel better to ruin Peggy's day?" The anger in his voice was unconcealed.

"What do *you* know? Everything in *your* life is great." Kelly allowed the bitterness to pour out of her. She had ruined everything anyway. Greg wouldn't even want her for a friend after this.

His words were quick and hot. "I'll tell you what I know. You're a self-centered little idiot! You're so caught up in your own little world that you can't see other people have feelings, too. Peggy is a nice lady. She's never done anything mean to you, except marry your father! Did you ever stop to think that your father was lonely and needed a wife? Or that your little sister might want a mom? No! All you can think about is yourself."

Kelly shrank back against the wall as his angry words poured over her like hot oil. Her only thought was of escape. Giving a wounded little cry, she dashed off the porch and ran blindly into the woods. Tears swam in her eyes as sobs racked her body. She paid no attention to the limbs lashing her arms and legs. She rushed on as if being pursued by a wild animal. Gradually, her pace slowed. It had been a long, hot day, and she had not eaten since lunch. Her tired body refused to keep up the furious pace. Sobs continued to convulse her body as she walked through the woods.

Without realizing it, Kelly's wild flight had brought her to her favorite place at Camp Sonshine, a place she had discovered on one of her many morning rides on Crystal. Nestled between two stately oak trees was a lush carpet of fragrant grass. A few late-summer wildflowers still decorated three of its borders. The remaining border of her refuge were the gently lapping waves of the lake. Camp was out of sight, and the sighing wind covered up any sounds of voices.

Throwing her fatigued body down on the welcoming carpet, she cried until there were no more tears left in her body. Her eyes were red and swollen, her nose stuffy. She finally sat up and leaned back against one of the guardian oaks. As she reviewed the events of the day, Kelly groaned aloud.

What had she done? she wondered. She had ruined everything in her life. Her father would be furious when he heard what she had said to Peggy. Peggy hadn't deserved those angry words. She had just been trying to help. Susan must think she was a real jerk for lying about being a Christian, and Greg would probably never want to see her again.

Resting her head against the rough bark of the tree, Kelly allowed the cool air off the lake to flow over her tired body. Little by little she relaxed. The only sounds were the quiet whispering of the wind through the leaves and the rhythmic music of the waves kissing the shoreline. A strange kind of peace began to creep into Kelly's heart. Not stopping to wonder where it came from, she just allowed it to blanket her being. She was only vaguely aware of the lengthening shadows and the rosy hue of the sky as the sun slid below the horizon.

Then a strange thing began to happen. It was almost as if there were a presence in the refuge with her. Slowly, the events of the last year played back in her mind. As if she were watching a movie, Kelly relived her father's courtship with Peggy. She saw the loneliness disappear from his face and joy and contentment take its place. She also saw his disappointment and anger every time Kelly had been rude or thoughtless to the woman he loved. One by one, Kelly remembered the kind things Peggy had done for her and the understanding ways she had handled Kelly's rebuffs.

Flashing to church, Kelly saw Greg's laughing eyes when they had first met. She could hear his voice saying that Jesus was his best friend. She could see the disappointment on his face the afternoon she had snapped at him about Peggy. And she could feel his hurt when she had yelled at him back at camp.

As the movie continued to play, Martin's voice reminded her that God loved her and wanted to be her best friend. She saw him walking around the Sunday school classroom, telling about how Jesus had died for her so she could have a personal relationship with him.

Susan flashed on the scene. Kelly could almost feel her arms around her. *It's your choice, you know, Kelly. Jesus is waiting for you to trust him enough to come to him on your own. He'll never make you.*

It's your choice . . . He's waiting . . . He'll never make you . . .

The movie stopped. Kelly gazed across the lake as the words echoed through her heart and mind. Funny. Not once had she felt any condemnation while the scenes were playing in her mind. There had just been a gentle voice whispering to her to look and see what her actions had done.

She knew what she'd done was wrong. The movie in her mind had shown her clearly the hurt and unhappiness she had caused her dad, Peggy, and even Greg. She had been selfish and self-centered, just like Greg had said. Yet, a quiet voice had been whispering while the movie had played, *I really do love you, Kelly. You've tried it your way and it didn't work. You're only more unhappy than you were. Give your life to me. You can trust me.*

Just as the first stars began to twinkle above Camp Sonshine, Kelly bowed her head and quit fighting. Her voice mingled with the whisper of the leaves and water. "Okay, Jesus. I give up. Take my life. I've done nothing but mess it up. Please forgive me for all the stupid things I've done." Looking up into the darkening sky, she searched for the right words. "Thank you for dying for me. I'm going to trust you from now on. Please help me straighten out all the dumb things I've done."

Kelly could still feel the presence. Slowly, a warmth began to fill her body. There were no fireworks or feelings of exuberance, but a calmness spread into her heart. Along with the calm came the conviction that she had a lot of making up to do. She knew God had forgiven her. Now she had to ask Dad, Peggy, Greg, and Susan to forgive her as well. Their love for her was so clear now. Her own bitterness had blocked her ability to see it.

Rising from her hiding place, Kelly strode purposefully down the trail to camp. The trail was dark, but she had no fear. She had ridden it many times, and she knew it would come out below the barn before turning back to the main camp. Glancing at her watch, she realized it was almost time for Bible study. Sure that Susan would be worried about her, she increased her pace to a slow jog.

Suddenly a horse's high-pitched call broke the still air. Crystal! Kelly remembered she had forgotten to let her out for the night. She was probably good and mad by now. She had not had to stay in all night for weeks. It would only take a minute to turn her out. Then she would head for Bible study.

As Kelly hurried through the darkening woods, she was engulfed with the pain of losing her horse. Remembering her promise to Jesus to trust him, she raised her eyes toward heaven and breathed a quick prayer, "I don't understand it, but I'm going to trust you." After a quick thought she added, "It sure would be great if you could work out some way for me to keep her."

As she drew nearer to the barn, Kelly realized that the trail was easier to see. There was a strange, orange glow in the air that illuminated her way. What could be causing it? she wondered. Breaking out of the woods into the pasture below the barn, she gasped in horror.

The barn was on fire! She could see flames licking through the main door and smoke was beginning to plume from the building in a big, dark cloud. Again, the high-pitched call of a horse split the night. It was followed by the scream of another frightened animal.

Crystal! She was in that inferno! Kelly began to race toward the barn. Stopping just a moment at the door, she turned and screamed with all her might in the direction of the camp. "Help! Fire!"

Then she turned and disappeared into the barn.

As Kelly ran into the burning structure, the blast of heat almost sent her reeling backward. Instinctively she dropped to the ground, remembering heat and smoke from fire would be less at ground level. She realized she had learned *something* from health class. The glow of the flames lit her way as she crawled toward Crystal's stall.

The fire seemed to be concentrated in the tack room for now. The wooden structure was old, though. Kelly knew it wouldn't last long.

Crystal's terrified scream split the night once more. Her stall was closest to the blaze, and she was moving frantically in her attempts to escape.

Kelly finally reached the stall door. Reaching up, she slid the latch back quickly. Taking a deep breath, she stood to her feet. The smoke and heat almost gagged her, but she knew if she crawled in, Crystal would be even more terrified. Sliding into the stall, she discovered the walls seemed to be blocking out some of the smoke. She was able to breathe easier in the confines of the enclosure.

"Okay, girl. You're going to be fine now, Crystal. I'm going to get you out of here. Take it easy now." Speaking as soothingly as her fright would allow, Kelly moved quickly to the terrified, black filly's head. Her fingers moved nimbly to undo the bandanna from around her neck. Thank goodness she had not removed it after the day's work.

Crystal screamed once more and then lowered her head toward Kelly's voice. Her liquid eyes shouted confusion and fear.

"Here we go, Crystal. I'm just going to wrap this around your eyes so I can get you out of here." Swiftly she wrapped the bandanna around the frightened horse's head and knotted it around the halter. Kelly knew that once the door was open, she would have to move fast. The blaze was moving closer and closer to the stall door. Taking a deep breath, she swung the door open and moved forward. Crystal hesitated for just a moment. Her trust for Kelly won, and she bolted from the stall. Feeling the heat, she plowed to a stop and reared in protest.

Kelly was frantic. "God, please help me." Her prayer spun in her mind as she tugged at the frightened horse. She was gagging from the smoke and was beginning to feel faint from the heat.

Crystal's hooves abruptly fell back to the ground. Taking a firmer grip on her halter, Kelly pulled her forward. Just a few steps and they broke out into the night. Flames split the sky around her. Kelly was aware of the screams of the terror-stricken horses still inside the inferno. She ran forward with the filly until they were a safe distance from the barn. Then she undid the bandanna and gave Crystal a slap on her neck.

"Run! Get away from here!" She watched for just a second as the horse bolted into the night. Turning, she disappeared back into the barn. The heat and smoke had become more intense. Kelly wrapped the bandanna around her nose and mouth and crawled as close to the ground as possible. The other horses were in stalls further from the fire. If she could get to them, she could let them out the back doors of their stalls that led into the paddock. They would be able to get far enough away from the fire to be safe. It would be easier to go around to the back of the barn to the stall doors, but the fire was spreading too fast. The roundabout way, over several fences, would give the fire time to spread. The only way to save the horses was to go through the fire again.

Kelly gave a muffled cry as a burning board fell in front of her. Looking up, she gasped. The roof was on fire! The whole building was burning. She knew she didn't have much time, but she couldn't leave the horses to die. In the thick smoke that was swirling around her, it was hard to see where she was going. Her groping hand hit the sharp edge of the feed bin and she cried out in pain. But her cry was one of victory also. The feed bin was right beside one of the sick horse's stalls. Slipping the latch back, Kelly fell into the stall.

Here, as in the other stall, there seemed to be a slight reprieve from the heat and smoke. Kelly moved quickly to avoid Lady's flying hooves. The mare was terrified. Easing to the back of the stall, Kelly pushed back the bolt on the other door. Fresh air poured into the stall as the door swung open. The fire hadn't reached the back of the barn yet. Lady seemed to sense safety lay within her reach. Kelly jumped back out of the way just in time to avoid being trampled by the big mare as she bolted out of the burning structure.

Glancing up, Kelly watched, horrified, as the timbers above Lady's stall exploded into flames. She didn't have much time. Running from the barn, she quickly undid the outside latch on Holly's stall and watched in relief as she disappeared into the darkness. Only one more to go.

Just a few steps, and she had reached Jason's stall. Tugging at the latch, she was dismayed to discover that it was stuck. Putting all of her weight into the task at hand, she was rewarded by its sudden movement. She knew she had lost precious moments. Looking up at the flames licking the sky, she breathed another prayer. She could hear sirens in the distance, but she knew they could not get there in time to help her. If Jason was going to live, it would be up to her.

Pulling the door open, Kelly waited for the rush of a frightened horse. Nothing. Peering into the stall, she saw that Jason was too terror-stricken to notice the open door. Flames were creeping along the top of his stall, and his terrified eyes were rolled back into his head. Kelly took a deep breath of the night air and flashed to his side. Whipping the bandanna from around her head, she covered his frightened eyes and tugged him forward. Now that he could not see the fire, his other senses told him there was fresh air flowing in. His terrified mind acted from pure instinct. Jason bolted for the door.

Kelly's tired body was not quick enough to avoid the impact of his body. As she tumbled to the side, she felt a searing pain shoot through her leg. A cry of agony escaped her cracked lips. She looked up into the flaming rafters and pulled her body toward the open door. A rafter crashed to the ground behind her just as she reached the night air. She was aware of hands reaching out to her and then darkness enveloped her body.

EIGHTEEN

I thought maybe you were planning on sleeping the whole day away."

Kelly turned her head to focus on the voice coming from the side of her bed. Where was she? The burning barn was no longer crashing down around her. She was lying in a cozy, soft bed in a bright, sunlit room. A fragrant breeze was causing the bright yellow curtains to dance in the air. Had she dreamed the whole thing? As her eyes focused on the source of the voice, she recognized the worried face of her father.

"Dad! What are you doing here?"

Her father smiled in relief at the sound of her words. "At least you're talking. I don't mind saying I was scared to death when Randy called me last night. The idea of your being in that burning barn will probably keep me awake for months."

"So it wasn't a dream. I wasn't sure." Kelly suddenly sat straight up in bed and grabbed her father's hand. "Crystal—is she okay?"

"Relax. You were a hero last night. All the horses are safe. Crystal is fine. She's in the paddock behind the hay barn, refusing to eat. Susan says she's worried about you."

Kelly laughed in relief and leaned back against the pillows. It hadn't been a dream. The burning barn...Crystal...Jason plowing over her...It had all really happened. Everyone was safe. That's all that counted.

Her father took a tighter hold on her hand and continued in a warm voice. "I'm proud of you, honey. I hope you don't make a habit of it, but what you did took real courage. Not many people would run into a burning barn. Randy said they would have lost those four horses if you hadn't gone after them. Someone heard your yell, but by the time anyone got there, the barn was almost gone. Randy pulled you from that stall just as the roof crashed in." His face went white as he talked. Just a few seconds more and Kelly would have been dead. He leaned forward and gave her a warm kiss on the cheek.

"I thought I heard voices in here." Kelly looked up in surprise as Peggy entered the room. "I'm glad to see you're awake. You woke up for a few minutes last night while the paramedics were giving you oxygen, but they said you probably wouldn't remember. They gave you a sedative to make you sleep—said it would be the best thing for you."

As Peggy spoke, the rest of the night before came rushing back to Kelly's mind. *Her phone conversation with Peggy...Susan...Greg...giving her life to Jesus.* She had been on her way to ask everyone's forgiveness when she had discovered the barn. Kelly looked down in shame at the memory of what she had said to Peggy just the night before.

"Peggy. About last night..."

Peggy held her hand up to stop her words as she walked over to the bed. "We can talk about that later. Right now I just want you to relax and get strong. How does a shower sound? I had Tina bring you some fresh clothes. All they could do last night was pour you in this bed."

Suddenly the most important thing in the world was to tell Peggy and her father about what had happened last night. Kelly opened her mouth eagerly.

"How's my little hero?" Kelly turned her head at the sound of Randy's voice. Randy and Susan both had their heads poked around the edge of the door as if they were afraid she was contagious.

Kelly laughed at the expressions on their faces. "Come on in. As long as you don't mind the smell of smoke. I'm just beginning to realize I stink pretty bad. It doesn't seem to bother my parents."

Kelly saw Peggy and her father exchange glances. This was the first time she had ever referred to Peggy as one of her parents.

Susan strode into the room and sat down on the edge of the bed. Kelly's gasp of pain caused her to shoot back up to a standing position. "Kelly, I'm so sorry. I forgot all about your ankle. Please forgive me."

"My ankle?" Kelly looked at her father questioningly. The sudden pain that had shot up her leg when Susan sat down had been a surprise.

"You just sprained it, honey. It happened when Jason bolted out of his stall and ran into you. The paramedics wrapped it last night and said it should be good as new in three to four weeks. They're almost positive it's not broken, but they said we should take you to get it x-rayed, just to make sure. We have some crutches here for you to get around on."

Kelly sighed in relief. "If that's all that happened, I guess I'm pretty lucky."

Everyone's face whitened at the prospect of what could have happened if Randy had not been there to pull the girl out of the collapsing structure.

Randy forced a light tone, "We're all thankful that you're okay. We owe you a lot, Kelly." A briskness crept into his voice. "We have a whole camp waiting to know if you're okay. It's eleven now. Do you think you could make it to lunch by noon? I'll send the camp station wagon down to bring you and your folks up. It would mean a lot to everyone if you could make it."

"Don't you think that's a little soon? She's been through so much already. She needs some time to relax." Peggy's worried words filled the room.

Kelly's father stood up and put his arm around his wife. This time it didn't bother Kelly. It was nice to know Peggy still cared after last night. "Honey, if Kelly feels up to it, I think she should go. There are a lot of people concerned about her. Not to mention that boyfriend of hers who has been hanging around on the porch since six o'clock this morning."

Kelly barely heard Peggy's reluctant words of agreement. *Greg was worried about her.* Maybe she hadn't totally blown it last night. She had so much to tell all of them.

• • •

Kelly shifted her weight on the crutches and looked at her watch impatiently. "Dad, let's go ahead and walk up there. The kids are all going into lunch now. I don't want to be the last one in the dining room."

Kelly's father spoke soothingly, "Randy will be here with the wagon in a minute. The paramedics said to stay off your ankle as much as possible for the first few days."

Kelly missed the conspiring look that her father and Peggy exchanged over her head because her attention was drawn to the dust of the station wagon in the distance. Her heart was pounding with nervousness. She would be seeing Greg for the first time. He had been worried about her, but that didn't mean she had a chance of ever being his girlfriend after what had happened by the pay phone last night.

Kelly was aware that the dining room was full as she made her way up the sidewalk with her parents and Randy. It was unusually quiet, though. As Randy swung the door open for her to move into the crowded room, the whole group erupted into a loud cheer. It took several minutes for the cheering and clapping to die down. Then Susan jumped up on the stage and, with microphone in hand, led the entire camp in a rousing version of "For She's a Jolly Good Fellow."

Kelly fought the tears that threatened to overwhelm her. All of this for her! She glanced up as her father put an arm around her.

"I'm proud of you, honey."

If it hadn't been for the crutches, Kelly would have thrown her arms around him. It had been so long since she had felt the special closeness they had shared for so long. "I love you, Dad."

Kelly could see him fighting the mist in his eyes. "I love you too, Kelly."

Kelly was not aware that Randy had moved up on the stage and taken the microphone from Susan. "Okay, everybody. I think she got the message. What she did last night was a very courageous and wonderful thing. Camp Sonshine will always be indebted to her. How would everyone like to hear a word from our own resident hero?"

The camp broke out in cheers again. Kelly felt panic well up in her body. "Dad, I can't! What will I say? I can't talk in front of all these people."

Her father gave her a comforting squeeze, but offered no way out. "You can do it, honey. Anyone who can run into a burning barn to save horses can stand up in front of a group of campers and her friends and talk. Go on up there. The Lord will help you."

The Lord will help you. Those words no longer filled her with resentment. The Lord was now her friend and savior, too. She had wanted everyone to know how she had changed. Maybe this was God's way of giving her the chance to tell them. Kelly moved carefully through the maze of tables on her crutches. As she stood on the stage, her resolve almost deserted her when she looked down at the sea of faces staring up at her. Taking a deep breath, she began talking.

"Thanks a lot for this. I don't know that what I did was so brave. Most of you here would have probably done the same thing if you had been the one to find the fire. I'm just glad all the horses are safe! Saving the horses was a pretty important thing, but it wasn't the most important thing that happened in my life last night. As long as I'm up here, I'd like to tell you about it."

Kelly waited a few seconds for the murmur of surprise to die down and then continued, "I came to Camp Sonshine under false pretenses. In other words, I lied to get the job. You're supposed to be a Christian to be able to work here, and when I came here I wasn't. I just wanted the job so bad, I was willing to say and do anything to get it. Susan, I want you to know how sorry I am I lied to you."

She paused for a moment and looked the head wrangler squarely in the eyes. Susan gave her a gentle smile and encouraging nod. Taking strength from Susan's support, Kelly continued, "I knew about Jesus Christ, but I had a lot of bitterness and anger inside. I didn't want to have anything to do with him. You see, my mother died several years ago from cancer. A few months ago my dad got remarried. I was afraid of the change in my life, so I made a vow to never accept my stepmother. She's really a wonderful person, but I thought nobody cared how I felt. In the middle of all this my father became a Christian—my stepmother already was. That just meant more change, so I vowed never to accept Jesus either. My anger and bitterness have really messed things up. Yesterday it all kind of came to a head, and I really blew it. I yelled at Megan because I was upset at something else. I blew up at Susan when she was just trying to help. I blasted my stepmother on the phone. And then I was hateful to

Greg. I realize now how wrong I was, and I want to tell everyone how sorry I am."

Kelly's eyes were swimming with tears, and she was afraid to look toward her father and Peggy. "Last night, Jesus showed me how much I'd hurt the people I love the most. But you know, he wasn't mean about it. He was very gentle. I felt his love the whole time he was showing me the way I really was. I realized that I had been running in the wrong direction the whole time. I was running from the very person who could help me make sense out of all the change in my life. Anyway, I quit running and accepted Jesus into my life last night. I'm going to trust him from now on. I think, with his help, all of this change will turn out to be good."

Kelly finally looked up into the crowd and found Greg staring right at her. His face lit up in a big grin, and he gave her the thumbs-up signal. He wasn't mad at her. In fact, the expression in his eyes conveyed a promise she had been waiting a long time for. Kelly's heart skipped a beat, and her face lit up in a big grin of its own.

Randy cleared his throat and moved up to take the microphone from her. Putting his arm around Kelly, he pulled her close to his side. His eyes were suspiciously moist as he smiled down at her. "Thanks, Kelly. What you did just now took as much, or maybe more, courage than what you did in the barn last night. I hope all of you out there really listened to what she had to say. Change is a scary thing, and it happens to all of us at some time in our lives. Jesus loves us and wants to go through the changes with us. He doesn't promise to make things better right away. He is there to walk through it with us and carry us when we can't make it on our own."

Randy's presence gave Kelly the courage to look over at her father and Peggy. A warm glow spread through her body at the looks of love and pride on both of their faces. Everything was going to be okay. She had really blown it, but Jesus was already working it out. Kelly knew there would still be adjustments to be made as a family, but at least they would all be working on it together now.

The director's next words pulled Kelly's attention back. "Susan, I think it's time to present Kelly with our token of appreciation."

Kelly looked up at him in surprise. Token of appreciation? She didn't expect anything for what she had done. After all, Crystal was safe. What more could she want?

Susan faced Kelly as she took the microphone. "What you did last night was a wonderful thing. The four horses that were in the barn were very valuable. Their deaths would have been not only a great tragedy, but a large financial loss as well. Randy got on the phone this morning with all the members of the board of directors, and everyone was in agreement that something very special should be done for you. It didn't take us very long to decide what that 'something' would be. It's no secret how much you love Crystal. From the minute that black beast exploded onto this camp, there has been a special relationship between you two. It's as if you two were meant to be together. Randy's wife agreed she would hate to be the one to keep you two apart."

Kelly could hardly breathe. What was Susan saying? Would she be able to buy Crystal after all?

Susan's eyes were dancing with laughter as she continued, "You'll have to figure out another way to spend the money from this summer. On behalf of Camp Sonshine, I would like to present Crystal to you as your very own horse!"

As the room burst into cheers once more, Kelly could do nothing but stand and stare at the grinning head wrangler. Had she heard her right? The camp was *giving* Crystal to her?

A shout of laughter from the campers caused Susan to take Kelly's shoulders and turn her toward the window. Unknown to Kelly, Greg had slipped out at a signal from Randy. Now he was standing outside the dining hall, holding on to a prancing black filly with a huge red bow tied around her neck.

Kelly turned to Susan with tears streaming down her face. "Thank you so much."

"Thank *you*. Y'all were meant to be together. Now get out there with your horse!"

Book #2
A Matter of Trust

Living with a new parent is a lot harder than Kelly thought it would be. God changed Kelly's heart, but now she's finding it difficult for her actions to follow. Kelly and Peggy's relationship is put to the ultimate test when Crystal almost dies. Will Kelly open up to her stepmom when she needs her most?